IRON JACK RIDES

Senator Gwin returns to San Francisco weary and dejected, having failed to convince Congress to subsidise his dream of a fast mail service from Missouri to Sacramento — the Pony Express. However, cattleman Iron Jack — former Texas Ranger and guerrilla fighter — reckons there's another way . . . Gwin sends him East to seek the investment of freight magnate Will Russell. But Iron Jack had best watch his step: Kansas and Nebraska have a bounty on his head — for murder!

Books by Gordon Landsborough
in the Linford Western Library:

THE BANDAGED RIDERS
UNION SOLDIER

GORDON LANDSBOROUGH

IRON JACK RIDES

Complete and Unabridged

LINFORD
Leicester

First published in Great Britain in 1952
as
The Pony Express by Mike M'Cracken

First Linford Edition
published 2016

A catalogue record for this book is available
from the British Library.

ISBN 978–1–4448–2897–9

Published by
F. A. Thorpe (Publishing)
Anstey, Leicestershire

Set by Words & Graphics Ltd.
Anstey, Leicestershire
Printed and bound in Great Britain by
T. J. International Ltd., Padstow, Cornwall

This book is printed on acid-free paper

1

Close on four on a dark afternoon in December, 1859, the Southern Overland Mail coach trundled down Mortimer Street in San Francisco.

Though it ran regularly, these days, out through Monterey and Los Angeles and then across by the Santa Fe trail to St. Louis, it still held interest for this lusty, thriving, but isolated community on the Pacific Coast, and people came crowding out on to the board sidewalks to watch it come in. The driver, who was a proud man, in spite of bleary, bloodshot eyes and a long-weathered face, put on a great show of shouting and whip-cracking, and then pulled in his team of spent, blowing horses to a halt outside the stage-line company's office.

The passengers dismounted stiffly because the steady norther, blowing

1

over the mighty Sierra Nevada peaks, had chilled them as they sat cramped inside the draughty coach all that long way up the wintry, Californian coast. Luggage was thrown off, and a sack of mail from the East was picked up and carried to the primitive wooden building that was San Francisco's post office. The crowd followed, their hopes suddenly awakened by the thought that that sack might contain some message from someone long remembered but perhaps almost a continent's width away.

One of the passengers, a heavy, determined-looking man of middle age, strode into the stage-line company's office and asked the clerk what chance there was of getting a conveyance out to Sacramento. The clerk, a thin fellow, gaunt of face behind a five-day stubble, answered, laconically, maybe there'd be a coach going out in the morning, but he couldn't say for sure.

Then his casual glance lifted from some torn and dirty way-bills and he saw the face of the passenger, and his manner changed.

'Senator Gwin?' In that dark, crowded office, with its light-excluding stacks of merchandise for collection and outward shipment, it wasn't easy to identify any face.

The passenger nodded. The clerk became cordial — overwhelmingly so. 'Senator,' he said assuringly, 'there'll be a coach moving out at eight for Sacramento. You don't need to worry about gettin' a place. You tell me where you're stoppin' overnight, an' I'll be round personally in the mornin' to waken you.'

Senator Gwin thanked him. He sounded tired. He also sounded defeated, like a man who feels he has tried too long and now it's time he gave up.

He started to go out on to the street again, and now the clerk came up quickly behind him, his eyes excited, his thin jaws moving in quick rhythm on a plug of tobacco. Some of the men hauling cases into the building saw the excitement of the clerk, looked at the object of his interest, recognized the senator and promptly left the cases, and came up in eager support of the clerk.

Senator Gwin, about to turn down the broken board sidewalk, became suddenly conscious of the interest of the three men and turned.

His eyebrows bushed; his voice growled up an abrupt: 'Well?'

The clerk shuffled his feet awkwardly, then came straight out with it. 'How'd it go, senator? Did you — win?'

Gwin seemed to droop and his body appeared to deflate in a long, weary sigh. Then his head shook slowly, a complete answer in itself. 'Nope,' he told them. 'Reckon I lost. They just laughed at me, back East.' He sighed again, like a man reluctant to part with his dreams. 'Guess we'd all better forget about it. I guess it never stood a chance from the start.' And with that he stamped wearily away in search of a hotel for the night.

The clerk watched him go, and alongside him stood the freight hands. 'I'd ha' thought he'd have done it,' the clerk said morosely. 'Bill Gwin sure has got a tongue in his head — got tongue enough to talk even Congress into doin' things, I'd have thought. But maybe for once they wouldn't listen to reason.'

Reluctantly they all turned, like men saying goodbye to something long-cherished; and it was almost as though they were turning their backs on what could have been a bright excitement but for the senator's words . . .

A man barred their way into the office. He was tall and lean, thin-legged in the narrow trousers that tucked into riding boots. He wore the short, heavy coat of leather that told at once he was a man connected with cattle, and his hat had the wider brim adopted in states where the fierce sun had to be kept from the eyes.

'I heard a name,' the cattleman said, and his voice had the leisurely drawl of a Missouri man. 'Senator Gwin, wasn't it?'

The clerk stopped chewing, spat a brown line down an unoffending door post, and nodded. 'Yeah. That was the senator. He's just come in from Washington by the Overland.'

The cattleman pushed back his hat. His was the young-old face that was familiar everywhere in the hard West at the time — weathered a red-brown by constant exposure to torrid sun and almost unceasing wind, firm-jawed, level-eyed and resolute. The face of a man who lived hard, who knew danger when he saw it, and was prepared to tackle it.

'He didn't have no luck?' The cattleman stood aside to let the clerk enter. Wearily, as if heavily disappointed in something, the freight shifters bent over their cases.

'Them damn' boneheads said no,' the clerk said angrily, and stamped back to his seat behind the counter. He didn't know that young-old cattleman in the doorway, but he knew that he didn't need to go into details with him. The name of Senator Gwin stood for one thing — a project that had fired the imagination of all men in that new State of California — and the cattleman would know as much about it as he, the stage-line clerk.

Now, the clerk thought, he'd know that the Pony Express was doomed as a project — damned by a cynical, stay-back-East bunch of Congressmen. The thought made him furious. He'd wanted to see that line of fast mail riders in action over the American continent. Why, it would have been like having a race meeting to brighten their lives every day! They'd have been able to have bets on it, and there'd have been jobs for a lot of lightweight riders like himself . . .

He was just becoming highly critical of a set of crudely-written bills — was just about to hurl them in a screwed ball into a corner, to the ultimate despair of the owner of the freight — when he heard that young cattleman say, softly: 'I reckon there's another way . . . mebbe — without Congress.'

The clerk looked up, hope returning

to his thin face. His mouth opened to say something, but the cattleman turned and went away, following the direction of the senator.

'You hear that, you fellars?' called out the clerk excitedly to the freight hands. 'There's a guy thinks he c'n start the Pony Express another way — without Congress!'

The three stage-line hands looked at each other with shining eyes for a moment, and then turned to stare after that tall, lean, leather-coated man. And that night every man in San Francisco knew that there was still a chance for the Pony Express, the dream child of Senator William M. Gwin.

*　*　*

Gwin had difficulty in finding a place that would take him in for the night. California had more tents than solid buildings during that winter of '59. Just ten years before, Marshall had discovered gold in the bed of the American fork of the Sacramento River; in those ten years hundreds of thousands of people had come from all corners of the earth to try their luck in the diggings — and still they came. San Francisco just couldn't accommodate them all.

Then Gwin tried the Bedrock, was recognized and taken in. Gratefully he sat down for a meal in the elegant dining-room that was all mirrors and red plush — and had cost a fortune to bring round from Galveston by clipper.

He wasn't to be left in peace, however. Other patrons of the dining-room recognized him, and they shoved their plates up towards his end of the long table and began an eager questioning about his trip to Washington.

Senator Gwin made half-responses for a time, and then grew impatient. Finally he laid down his knife and fork and said, with grim good-humour: 'All right, I c'n see I won't get no peace until you know everything. Okay, I'll tell you. I went to Congress an' tried to get them to sponsor a fast mail service

9

from the railhead on the Missouri to Sacramento, here on the Pacific Coast.'

His heavy face became flushed as he remembered those meetings with the unsentimental Congressmen.

'I told 'em the United States had in California the finest an' richest country anywhere in the Union. And I told 'em there wasn't a road worth a damn into the state, an' sometimes we had to wait two months, three months — aye, an' more — to get our letters from the East.'

He took a drink of rye coffee that was bitter to his mouth after the good drink of the East. Mail had to come via Panama, and the best that could be expected was twenty-two days for delivery. The steamships had improved the service, though they weren't always as fast as the old, graceful Yankee clippers, but it was still a hardship to have to wait maybe half a year to get a reply to a letter.

'I told 'em we wanted overland mail delivery. I said a chain of riders could carry mail two thousand miles across the continent, handin' on from man to man. I said it could be done, if Congress would pay $5,000 for each trip.'

Some miner at the end of the table called: 'That's a lot of money, Senator.'

Gwin called back: 'It wouldn't be lost. Run right, in time the Pony Express could pay its way. What would you give to be able to send your mail right across America in ten days or less? Five dollars a time?'

Five dollars! That was nothing in a state where men earned sixteen dollars a day in raw gold, just tilting a cradle in the tributaries that ran down from the Sierra Nevadas.

Gwin repeated dogmatically: 'It'd pay all right, friend.'

'But Congress didn't think so?' A quiet-looking man next to Gwin opened his mouth to speak the words. Gwin shook his head sorrowfully.

'Nope. They just laughed at me. They said it wasn't possible to run a pony service the way I said.' His voice growled away, angrily: 'Just a durn lot of city folks, them Congressmen! They don't know what a horse c'n do, that's the trouble.'

He lifted his fork over a giant steak, then dug at it savagely. A crowd had collected to listen to him, standing with their glasses just inside the dining-room doorway. Gwin was about to raise a choice piece of cow beef to his lips, when the spectators at the doorway parted to let through a girl and a big, well-dressed young man.

The girl flew across to the dining-table, calling: 'Uncle!'

Senator Gwin rose clumsily to his feet, surprised to see his niece there in that not-too-reputable hotel. 'Why, Ann!' he exclaimed in surprise. Then his gaze travelled over her shoulder, meeting the eyes of the girl's escort. At once his own eyes narrowed and became grim, and his face hardened. With an abrupt nod to the big, easy-mannered young man, he turned back to his niece.

'Anythin' wrong, Ann?' he asked gently, for he could see there were signs of grief on the girl's face . . . as if she had been crying.

She nodded, dropping her eyes, and he thought she would cry again. She was a pleasant, neatly-dressed girl, prettier than most who had survived the perils of the trail to get to California.

'It's mother,' she whispered.

Senator Gwin caught her hand quickly. Her mother — that was his beloved sister back in Kansas City. 'Is she — dead?'

Ann lifted eyes that were brimming with anguish. 'I don't know. A letter came with yesterday's sea mail to Sacramento. Mother has been ill all summer. The letter talks of a decline.' The girl wrung her hands, knowing what that could mean. 'It urged me to come home, to be with her in case — in case — '

'In case she dies,' thought Senator Gwin, and his face was ashen grey. He had been within two hundred and fifty miles of his sister on this trip back east. Maybe even less, shortly after leaving St. Louis and the Mississippi. He had been tempted to take horse and ride north to see her, but his trip to Washington had taken time, and he had been anxious to return quickly to attend to urgent affairs in California, so he had kept to the uncomfortable, lurching, winter-cold stage-coach all the way across the continent.

'You're goin' right now?' the senator asked gently. The other diners were listening, but their silence was respect for the girl's and her uncle's grief at the moment.

'Yes. I packed some things the moment I read the letter.' The girl lifted her eyes to her uncle's, and now she was crying softly. 'Oh, uncle, that letter took twenty-one weeks to reach me. In that time — '

Senator Gwin held her hand tightly, as if to give her courage to bear the thought. Twenty-one weeks — his sister could have died in that time. He thought, savagely: 'That's how we suffer, we pioneers here in the West. The East doesn't give a damn about us, though it's our gold that's helpin' to make America the richest country in the world. Why should we have to wait over five months for vital mail, when a relay of horsemen could get it through to the Golden State in a week and a half?'

He heard his niece say: 'The steamer ran aground on a sand bar off Florida, and had to put into St. Petersburg for repairs. That's why it was so late.'

The big, well-dressed young man who was her escort moved up behind her at this and put his hand familiarly on her shoulder, to console her. Gwin's eyes lifted angrily, but he said nothing at the gesture.

The big, over-heavy young man saw the look, but smiled easily, as if not worried by the senator's dislike of him. He wore the black frock coat that indicated respectability at that time in the West, with a white shirt that was really white, and a bow tie such as gamblers affected.

He looked cityfied, but he carried himself in a way that made men realize that he wasn't soft. His hands were smooth and uncalloused, but they were big and strong and looked like hands that had once performed heavier work in the past. There was weight on his broad shoulders under the smooth black cloth, but big muscles were there, too, even though they were going a little too fat now with recent disuse.

And he had a way of looking at men with his head rather lowered, so that his eyes glinted up through thick brows, in a way that was at once boldly truculent and challenging.

Rolly Weyte had made good on the diggings. He had three good claims which he nowadays paid men to work for him, and it was said that he had a quarter of a million stacked away in gold in the Western Union Bank.

But there were men who said that

only one of the claims was rightfully his . . .

'We came into town,' Rolly Weyte said easily, as if deliberately showing his contempt for the senator's dislike of him, 'and we heard you'd just come in aboard the Overland, so we came to find you.'

A lean, hardy cattleman in a thick leather coat had come pushing his way through the crowd at the door. When he heard Rolly Weyte's voice, however, he halted, and the puckered brow of that strong, brown face suggested that the man thought he had recognized the voice.

Gwin asked: 'Where are you stayin'? The Royal?' The girl nodded, her back to the room, wiping away her recent tears. 'I'd like to go with you, Ann, but — ' Gwin shrugged helplessly. 'I'm just in, and I reckon I'd better get my business attended to before I start gallivantin' back East again.'

Then he asked a question that brought a startling answer: 'You goin' out with the Overland tomorrow?' That would be the way he had come, the only stage route across America at that time to California — via South California and the Santa Fe trail.

Ann shook her pretty head, and a look of obstinacy clouded her young face. 'No, uncle. Mr Weyte is travelling with one of Awker's freight trains as far as Virginia City, and he's promised to find me a place.'

Gwin exploded: 'But it's mid-winter, and that means crossing the Nevadas.' His eyes lifted, to blaze across at the easy-smiling Weyte. Plainly his dislike of the prosperous mine-owner made him anxious to find any excuse to prevent his niece from travelling in the man's company.

'The train'll get through,' smiled Rolly Weyte pleasantly. 'And your niece will be perfectly safe, I promise you,' he added, and there was a faint note of mockery in his voice.

'I shall be all right,' urged Ann. 'Don't worry about me, uncle. If I go by the Oregon Trail I can be in Kansas in a matter of three weeks or less. If I go by Overland coach, it'll take me a month to work my way up to Kansas City, and — and that might make me too late.' She stopped, gulping back a fresh onslaught of tears.

The young, wiry cattleman had stepped carefully round the dining-table, so that he was able to look into the cool, insolent-smiling face of the gold-mine owner. His brow was still corrugated, but now it was uncertain. He was thinking: 'Wonder what this fellar'd look like behind a beard and in workin' clothes?' Yet he felt that face and voice tied together in his memory, and they were connected with horrifying events in his mind.

'All right,' agreed Gwin shortly. 'I know how you feel, with that letter so long in reachin' you. But I rely on you, Mr Weyte, to see that no harm comes to my niece.' His chin was up and pugnacious, and he was telling the gold-mine owner as plain as words that there'd be a powerful lot of trouble for him if harm did befall the girl.

The spectators sensed the antagonism and looked for Weyte's reaction, but the big young fellow just laughed and said nothing at the senator's words. It took some doing, in California in those wild days, to buck against a man as powerful as a United States senator, but every line of Weyte's face showed his contempt for the distinguished older man, and plainly Gwin didn't like it.

Ever since Ann had come to California to find health away from the dust of Kansas, Rolly Weyte had tried to woo her. Gwin didn't like the man, didn't like the whispers that went around regarding the mine-owner's methods, and he had tried to protect his niece against Weyte's advances. But Weyte was a bold and persistent admirer, and it seemed that during the senator's absence back East he had made progress. Gwin thought grimly: 'That was a stroke of luck for Weyte, him goin' to Virginia City just when Ann needed to go quickly through to Kansas.'

His eyes shifted slightly, so that they took in a new picture. It was of a leather-coated, tough-looking *hombre* who was watching Weyte's face as though his life depended on it. Gwin's eyes became suddenly interested. This stranger didn't seem to go for Weyte, either, which was a point in his favour. He wondered who the man was, what he had against the mine-owner.

Then the lean, hardy cattleman turned and met the senator's interested gaze. At once the bold, brown face seemed to go blank, as if deliberately he had put up shutters to screen his mind and keep it private from other people's pryings. Weyte's eyes flickered across, and for one second it seemed that they dilated slightly — and then he was his old, normal, mocking self again.

Senator Gwin asked, courteously: 'Did you want to speak to me, stranger?'

'Not if it wasn't a good moment,'

said the cattleman, and his eyes shot back, quick and hard, to Weyte's face . . . but there was nothing there to see but the smooth, confident smile that was insolence itself.

The senator said: 'This moment is as good as any, I guess.' He felt that he wanted to know more about this stranger, wanted to know what he had against this mine-owner whom he, Gwin, detested and yet in a way feared.

The cattleman looked him straight in the eye. 'I'm told you didn't go down well with Congress, senator.'

Gwin's face seemed to darken, as if to be reminded of that ill-fated trip back East hurt him. 'I didn't,' he retorted shortly. 'I was a fool to have gone all that way, I reckon.' He shrugged. 'Reckon the Pony Express will be flung into my face as long as I live — an old fool's crazy pipe-dream,' he ended, his voice bitter and cynical.

'Yeah? Mebbe not such a pipe-dream, senator.' Something in the way the cattleman spoke brought sudden life back into the senator's eyes.

'What do you mean, stranger?'

The cattleman sat down on a seat next to the girl, so that he could talk on level terms with the senator. The girl turned so that she could look into that strong, brown face — the face of a man who could dare and do things. She seemed to be fascinated by what she saw there, by the way he spoke, so coolly and deliberately.

'Senator, it was plumb foolish to expect Congress to authorise anythin' new like a Pony Express stretchin' near on a couple of thousand miles.' Gwin nodded slow agreement. 'But I reckon I know a fellar who'd do it for you, if you went an' talked a long time to him.'

At his words there wasn't a sound in that dining-room; every eye was fixed on the lean, young cattleman. The Pony Express was something the entire state had set its heart on; to be within ten days' mailing distance of the East meant an end to the feeling of isolation that was common to all settlers in

California, and its worth in expediting business — especially in ordering new, much-needed goods — would be incalculable. So now they waited breathlessly to hear the solution propounded by this stranger.

Gwin said, hopefully: 'This fellar — what's his name, stranger?'

'Russell. Will Russell.'

'Will Russell?' Senator Gwin repeated. 'I don't know that I've ever heard of him.' His eyes watched the cattleman narrowly, suspecting that once again his hopes would be dashed, and so he didn't allow himself to become buoyed up by the stranger's words.

'If you lived in Utah, over them hills, or anywhere between there and Kansas, you'd know Will Russell,' the cattleman drawled confidently. 'He's the fellar that got the contract to haul supplies for the army in the Mormon war, a coupla years back. They said he had four thousand wagons, five thousand men, and forty thousand oxen on that job alone.'

He leaned forward impressively. 'Senator, that Russell fellar's big — he thinks big an' he does everything big. He's the fellar to back this Pony Express idea of your'n. An' I think he'd do it, if it was put to him. He's the biggest freight hauler between Salt Lake City an' Leavenworth; he's got way stations all along the Oregon Trail, through Kansas, Nebraska, Colorado, Wyomin', into Utah. Why, he's two-thirds of the way across to California, an' I reckon he's itchin' for a chance to spread his business to the Pacific Coast. The Pony Express would give him his chance.'

Senator Gwin looked startled. Then a faint flush began to rise to his cheeks, and there was a look in his eyes as of a man who dares to resurrect a cherished idea once again.

'Stranger, you talk a powerful lot of sense,' he breathed, and at the words there was a sigh from that crowded dining-room, as if the spectators had been hoping to hear such a verdict from the senator. Now they pressed closer, intent and listening.

The girl, so near to the cattleman, exclaimed: 'Oh, how wonderful! If only you're right!' Her eyes were shining, forgetting her own troubles for the moment because it seemed that her uncle's hopes were perhaps to be realized after all — and she knew how much that Pony Express idea meant to the progressive-minded senator.

The leather-coated man shifted his gaze, so that his calm blue eyes looked even bluer so close to him. He drawled, confidently: 'Ma'am, I'll be right, you see if I'm not.'

Rolly Weyte, big, black-coated, smooth-smiling, watched those two young faces so close to each other at the table, but what his thoughts were no one could guess from his countenance. There was a lot of gambler in Weyte, and he could think things without revealing them on his face.

It seemed that there was a faint reluctance on the part of the rugged-looking cattleman to remove his gaze from those bright shining eyes before him and return to his business with the senator.

The senator asked: 'Do you know Russell — personally?'

'Yep. Like a few thousand other people in the Middle West,' drawled the cattleman. 'Everyone knows Will Russell, an' his partners, Alex Majors and Waddell.'

The senator leaned forward again, earnestly. 'Look, stranger, what I'm gettin' at is this — I'm new in from Washington, and I can't take any more trips back East until I've got some important state business cleared up. How about you goin' to Leavenworth an' puttin' the proposition before the Russell firm?'

'Act for you?' The cattleman was surprised. Then humour came to his eyes. 'That sure comes of stickin' your nose into other people's business.'

'What's your business? Cattle?'

'Yep. I drive cattle up from the Rio Grande through El Paso an' San Diego.

I keep hearin' of this Pony Express — want to see it in action myself, too, I reckon — an' when I heard Congress were down on the idea I thought of Will Russell an' how he might help you.'

'But how about my proposition?' persisted the senator. 'I'll pay your expenses if you'll take on the job.' He was thinking that this bold-looking, tough cattleman was just the type to represent him on such a deal. His eyes dropped to the cattleman's slim waist, revealed by the parted leather coat. A useful-looking Colt .45 was slung at the cattleman's side.

The cattleman was hesitating. Then the girl said: 'Please, mister, do take on the job. You don't know how much this means to my uncle — and to me.'

'To you?' The cattleman gave an old-fashioned little bow as he sat there, legs astride his chair. 'Ma'am,' he said gallantly, 'I reckon for that I'll have to take on the job.'

Then he rose. 'I'm drivin' cattle up to Sacramento, Senator. That's where you're headin', I reckon. I'll call on you in two-three days' time, when I'm through with this drive.'

He nodded to the senator, bowed slightly towards the bright-eyed girl, then turned to go. That brought him face to face with Weyte.

They faced each other momentarily, their eyes probing each other's. The mocking smile never left Weyte's face, but the cattleman's was hard and inscrutable as he looked at the mine-owner.

Then he turned away, and Weyte realized that he still didn't know if he had been recognized. The crowd parted to let the cattleman stalk through the doorway, and there was a murmur as he passed them and some of the men slapped him on the back as if to bring him good luck on his mission. Then he was gone.

The senator and his niece watched him go, and their eyes were shining. As the crowd became noisy again within the room, Gwin raised his voice.

'Let's all drink together. Maybe the Pony Express isn't as dead as I thought it was, thanks to that fellar!'

Over the hubbub that greeted his words, Weyte's mocking voice drawled: 'You don't know that *hombre*, Senator. Mebbe you're pinnin' hopes where they're not deserved.'

Gwin's eyes flashed challengingly. 'I know a straight man when I see one,' he retorted, and his manner said: 'And you're not straight, Rolly Weyte.' Weyte merely nodded good-humouredly. Gwin went on: 'That fellar somehow gives me confidence. He's — well, tough, but he's got intelligence. I think mebbe he's got the sand to pull this off where I failed.' And the senator wouldn't mind that; wouldn't mind this bold, young cattleman succeeding over his failure, for the Pony Express meant everything to him just now. All he wanted was to see California, this rich and vigorous young state, with the efficient postal communication that it sorely needed.

He called for another plate of food,

his own having gone cold. And then his niece spoke: 'It's curious, uncle. We never thought to ask his name, and he didn't offer to give it.'

The senator looked round the table quickly. 'Yes, that's right. We should have asked. Anyone know his name?'

For a moment no one spoke, every man looking at each other. Then Rolly Weyte broke the silence. He was walking towards the door, and already there was a plan in his mind.

'Next time you meet up with him, Senator,' Weyte said, 'try the name of Irons on him — Jack Irons.'

'Jack Irons?' A bearded prospector down the table suddenly exploded at the name. 'Jack Irons — the fellar they call Iron Jack all along the Rio Grande?'

If Jack Irons wasn't familiar to the men in that room, then Iron Jack was! There was a sudden upsurge of sound as men repeated the name and then began to speak of the man and his reputation. Iron Jack had commanded a troop of Texas Rangers after the war with Mexico, and his fame as a guerilla fighter had spread all across the West. So this was the celebrated Iron Jack, who had fought his way to Monterrey in Mexico to release captive Texans, men and women, and bring them after bitter days of rear-guard action safely to McAllen. His name would live on the Border for a long time as a result of that bold exploit.

'Yes,' smiled Rolly Weyte, halting by the crowd at the door. 'Iron Jack himself.' His eyes travelled back to the table; they lingered a second on the senator, and then rested on the girl's flushed, excited face.

'And if you think Iron Jack's a man to pin your hopes on, you've picked the wrong man.' He was talking to the senator, but his eyes, amused and cool, were on the girl.

Senator Gwin, irritated, not wanting to believe what he heard, snapped, 'Oh . . . and why?'

'Iron Jack daren't enter Kansas or Nebraska. There's a reward out for him there — for murder!'

Rolly Weyte left the Bedrock with those parting words. Outside, he hesitated a second, then pushed through the pressing throng of rough, noisy miners, out on the spree, until he came to the offices of the Awker Freight Corporation.

'Jud Awker in?' he asked at the counter. An old man, warming himself by a round, pot-bellied stove, jerked his head towards an inner office. Weyte nodded and walked through.

One way or another, he was determined to make sure of Iron Jack . . .

2

Senator William Gwin rode half-way to San Joaquin City in his anxiety to meet again the celebrated Border fighter, Jack Irons. That was two days later, when he anticipated that the cattleman would have returned to his herd in the San Joaquin Valley, and should by now be very close to Sacramento.

He drove out in his carriage, very elegant and unusual so far in the mining area, though plenty were being landed every week across in 'Frisco. When he came to the bridges, where the Sacramento River split into several courses across the rich, flat valley, he halted and sat for several hours watching the trail ahead.

Finally, close on evening, a miner trudging on foot to the diggings beyond Smith's Bar told him that a herd of a couple of thousand beeves was being bedded down for the night just outside San Joaquin.

Gwin hadn't wanted to trail so far away from his home — certainly not so late in the day — but his impatience was too much for him, and he whipped up his horses and went at a spanking trot across by the old, useless workings on the San Joaquin City road.

Jack Irons and a couple of punchers were making coffee as the senator came trundling along the rutty trail. Irons reached out for the can and waved the senator over.

'Guess you're in time for cawffee,' he said hospitably. The senator stood beyond the camp fire, looking at the blankets and saddles laid out for sleeping, and the sheets of waterproof that would have to serve as roof in case it rained.

'You live hard, Irons,' he found himself saying, then realized that he had spoken the cattleman's name. Irons didn't say anything to that. 'I'm gettin' too old for life on the trail,' he went on, speaking quickly to cover his mistake.

Irons poured out a mug of hot, steaming coffee for their guest. It was real coffee, as you'd expect from a cowboy, thick and strong and sweeter than sweet.

'It suits me,' drawled the cattleman. 'Though I reckon some day mebbe I'll feel like you old-timers, Senator, an' say I've had enough.'

The senator didn't sit beside the fire. Instead he looked at the tough punchers, preparing their evening meal, decided not to speak his mind in their presence, and instead addressed himself to the cattleman again.

'I'd like a word with you, Irons,' he growled, and jerked his head significantly.

'Sure.' The cattleman climbed stiffly to his feet, like a man who has spent a hard day in the saddle. 'There's a question I'd mebbe like you to answer, too, Senator.'

They moved away, to where a broken 'dobe wall told of a former Mexican or

Spanish residence of long ago. It gave them shelter from the cool, persistent north wind. Irons said, calmly: 'Where'd you get my name, Senator? I don't advertise it, normally.'

'Weyte told us who you were.'

'Weyte?' Jack Irons frowned. 'I don't know any guy called Weyte.'

'Rolly Weyte? He knew you. He came in with my niece.' Senator Gwin spoke as though he didn't like to couple Weyte with his niece even in speech, and it didn't pass unnoticed by the observant cattleman.

'Him? That's his name, is it? I used to know him as Rowlands.' Jack Irons' eyes came up to meet the senator's, and they were hard. 'Bet he had more to say about me than my name.'

The senator sighed. 'He did, Irons. He told us you were wanted for murder back in the Middle West, and that you wouldn't dare go back to Leavenworth to speak to Russell.'

Iron's eyes twinkled. 'That sounds suspiciously like you're tryin' to dare me to go, senator.'

'Well, dare you?'

'Sure. Why not? I reckon it's more'n five years since I lit out in a hurry for Texas — an' safety. I don't suppose there's many'll recognize me now — not in Leavenworth, anyway. Besides,' he added softly, 'there's someone back in Kansas City I'd like to see again.'

Senator Gwin was watching the cattleman closely while he was speaking, and he felt dissatisfied with what he saw. This cowpuncher was too cool in his talk about murder; he would have liked him better if he had made some attempt to excuse himself for whatever crime had been committed. But Irons didn't refer to the matter, though there was that faintly humorous glint in his eyes, as if he was conscious of what was going on in the senator's mind.

'Well, that's a relief, anyway,' the senator said. 'You're willin' to make the trip on my behalf and talk to Will Russell?' The cattleman nodded. 'I said I'd pay your expenses for you — ' The senator hesitated. It would be so easy for this cattleman to accept his money, go away and never be heard of again.

Jack Irons said, calmly, 'You don't have to worry, Senator. I'll collect my expenses when I bring back the news that Russell's okaying the Pony Express.'

Gwin flushed a little, ashamed to find that his thoughts were read so easily by this young cattleman. Jack Irons was no slouch when it came to handling men, he thought, and decided that was no bad thing with such a difficult task ahead of him.

The senator began to give details about the proposed Pony Express route, and Irons listened respectfully, because it was obvious that the senator knew the backlands like a book.

'Carson City, Virginia City, and then Salt Lake,' the senator told him, and then went into details about that desert route and the way through the Rockies. After that it would join the Oregon Trail at Fort Bridger, would cross Wyoming by Fort Laramie, and then along the

Platte through Nebraska to Kansas. St. Joseph would be the Eastern terminus of the run, because there it could connect up with the railroad from back East.

They talked until darkness was no more than an hour away, and then, reluctant even to leave talk of his beloved project, the senator stepped out from the shelter of the wall and began to walk across to his carriage. On the way he said: 'You'll follow that route, Jack.' He hesitated, then glanced quickly at his companion. 'An' you c'n do me another favour, as far as Virginia City, too.'

'Sure,' said Irons, cordially. 'Glad to oblige. Just say what it is.'

'Keep a watch-out for my niece,' Senator Gwin said gruffly. 'She's travellin' with some of Awker's wagons, an' I don't like her goin' off back East on her own.'

Irons held the horses, restive suddenly when they realized that the time for moving had arrived again, while the

40

old senator climbed heavily onto the high seat.

'Senator,' Irons said coolly, 'ain't that kinda remarkable, askin' a man wanted for murder to watch out for your niece?'

It jolted the senator, reaching forward for the reins, and he sat back and stared down at the hard-looking cattleman. Somehow he couldn't think of this man as a murderer; he didn't seem the killer type, for all his toughness.

He said, thoughtfully: 'Yeah, mebbe it is.' His head jerked up. 'Was it — a bad affair, that killin'?'

Irons shrugged. 'All killin's bad, I reckon.' Still he didn't talk about the details of the crime that was labelled against him.

Yet in some way the senator was satisfied.

'I don't know what happened — as a senator, I don't want to know, Jack,' he told him. 'All I c'n say is, I think I'd trust you with my niece before that smooth-tongued Rolly Weyte.'

'Rolly Weyte?' The languor left the

cattleman in an instant and he seemed fairly to bristle with hate. 'What about Weyte? Where is he? Don't tell me he's gone off with your niece?'

'That's just what I'm tellin' you.' The senator's voice was heavy. 'I couldn't stop it. She's got to go back to her mother in Kansas City quickly, an' Weyte, it turns out, is goin' to Virginia City an' offered to see her through the mountains.'

'Weyte?' breathed Irons. 'With that girl! My God!'

But the senator didn't hear those last words and could only guess at them. And in keeping them to himself, Iron Jack was being kind, not wanting to alarm the old man.

Abruptly Irons nodded. 'I'll watch out for the gal,' he said. 'If I come across her, I'll look after her.' And to himself he whispered: 'There's a lot of scores I'd like to settle with Rolly Weyte at the same time!'

Somehow it satisfied the senator, and when he said goodbye a minute later, he went home feeling unusually pleased. He had confidence in that lean, tough cattleman — was confident he'd put across this spectacular idea of a Pony Express when he met Russell, and at the same time he felt sure that he'd look well after his niece, now a day along the trail into the Rockies.

When he returned home a friend of his called to see him. He was the town marshal of Sacramento. The marshal said: 'There's talk that you're engagin' Iron Jack to act for you over this Pony Express, Bill.'

The senator said, levelly: 'What of it, Joe?'

The marshal shrugged. 'You'd better know first there's a reward out for him in Kansas of two hundred dollars, an' there's a bounty man here in Sacramento right now waitin' to pick him up an' take him back to Kansas an' claim the reward.'

The senator just said, laconically: 'He'll mebbe have to wait a long time,' for Irons' last words to him had been:

'I'll take the trail tomorrow. These boys'll see the beeves into Sacramento and save me my share of the money.'

As a senator it was wrong of him to feel sympathy with a man wanted for murder, but all the same that's how it was where Iron Jack was concerned.

When the marshal was about to leave, Gwin remembered to ask an important question. 'What's the charge agen Irons, Joe?'

The marshal said: 'Murder.'

'Sure, I know it's murder. But . . . what kind?'

'The worst.' There was no sympathy on the marshal's face as he picked up his hat. 'He killed a woman!'

For a long time afterwards Gwin stared out into the night, trying to resolve his thoughts. But all he could say was: 'I can't believe it. He's not the kind to kill anyone.'

And then doubt assailed him — doubt and horror. For he had consigned his beloved niece to the care of this man, and where his niece was concerned he couldn't take chances.

He rode out at first light to meet up with the herd again. When he reached it the punchers lifted their weatherbeaten faces and told him that Iron Jack had changed his mind the previous night — he'd collected blankets, ammunition and food, and ridden off while there was still light to see. He was in a hurry to catch up with the Awker wagon train, was all that he'd said to them, and with that the senator had to be content and return to his home.

* * *

Dawn found Jack Irons climbing the trail that led through the Sierra Nevada range via Carson City, in Nevada. He was already twenty miles from San Joaquin, near to where he had spoken with the senator the previous night, and the air was cold at this height in the bare, sparsely wooded hills, with their occasional live-oaks and straggling pines.

He had slept the night in a Mexican

'dobe house on the banks of a small stream — the house was but a single room, without glass to the window or board to cover the stamped earth floor, but it was better than sleeping out on the cold hillside, and Jack Irons merely thought he was lucky to find such a place after dark.

A breakfast of tortillas and meat lavishly covered with hot chile colorado sauce, was a good start to the chilly dawn, and he set off in good spirits, leaving a stammering Mexican to call *muchos gracias* for a mile along the road after him. Jack was generous, like most cattlemen, and the hardworking Mexican couldn't say that of all his visitors.

The cowpuncher had decided to take advantage of the last hour of light, the previous evening, and start off after the girl because he felt that he couldn't get to her side quick enough.

He knew there was a danger, with Weyte so close to her, but there was something more that called him urgently to her side that night.

His face had showed scarcely any feeling, that day in San Francisco when he had sat so close to her and looked into her shining, excited eyes. Yet inwardly he had been a sea of turbulent emotion, looking at her.

His hard life along the Border rarely brought him into contact with girls, and what girls he usually saw were the dark, coarse-haired beauties, too voluptuous for his fastidious taste. To sit, then, so close to that dainty, fair-haired girl had proved overwhelming. Almost every moment since the encounter he had been dreaming about her beauty, seeing in his mind's eye those shining blue eyes, that delicate fair skin . . .

But the moment the senator had left him, he had decided to ride off after the girl. Now he had been given an excuse to see her again and to speak to her, and all in one moment he couldn't get to her side fast enough.

By noon he was high in the pass that led over the mountains. There was snow glistening on the mountain peaks, and occasionally clouds of drifting flakes came rolling down the bleak mountainside, coating it a thin white almost down to where he rode the trail.

The cattleman didn't like the look of it. Usually the trail kept open until early in January, but this year it seemed heavy snow might be expected any time now. It would make heavy going for the Awker wagon train ahead.

He found signs of a considerable encampment shortly after noon, and guessed that here it was that the wagon train had halted for the night. That meant that he should overtake them by nightfall, with a bit of luck.

A thickening swirl of snow advanced down the trail towards him, engulfing him, and slowing his pace because of the need to fight against the driving whiteness. It lasted ten minutes or so, and then as suddenly lifted, having done no great harm to the trail.

Irons wiped the snow from his eyebrows and caught a glimpse of movement along the trail ahead of him. He saw two horsemen sheltering their horses close against a bluff, fifty yards off the trail, but as his eyes fell on thorn they pulled out and began to ride slowly along the rutted track ahead of him.

Within minutes he caught up with them, hunched in their coats against the biting wind. They turned in their saddles as he came up, and he found himself looking into impassive scrubby-chinned faces. He had an instant feeling of not liking them, but gave out the customary: 'Howdy, pards,' as he rode alongside. They grunted something in reply.

Jack Irons was no tenderfoot to be riding those trails, so that from the first he was watching them covertly, as he would have watched any chance-met riders along that lonely road. Too many bad characters had followed the trail of gold for a man to feel sure of his company in the lawless West.

They spoke but little in reply to his

questions concerning the wagon train ahead. They just said they hadn't seen anything of it.

Then Irons began to realize that the men were stealthily reining in their horses, so that his own could come through between them. When he realized what they were doing, his brain became suddenly alert, and his eyes all the more watchful.

They succeeded in their plan. Irons let his horse pass between them and even get in front.

Then he turned round — and there was a gun in his hand. They'd been looking at each other, nodding slightly as if signalling agreement upon some premeditated course of action. As he turned Irons saw the first movement of a hand reaching down for the cold blue butt of a large Navy Colt — then their startled eyes saw they had been outwitted.

Iron Jack's face was grim as he surveyed the pair. 'You think I was born yesterday?' he asked sardonically.

They began to bluster, asking him what he meant. So he told them.

'You were waitin' for someone to come up the trail, weren't you? You thought maybe you'd meet up with some miner an' lift his poke for him. But I came on, so you thought you'd stick me up instead — only I got wise to what you were after an' it's you that's lookin' down a gun muzzle now instead o' me.'

He caught the sudden swift interchange of glances and afterwards remembered and wondered at it. Almost it seemed to him that there was a slight expression of relief on their faces, but he couldn't see much for them to feel relieved about and he decided he had been mistaken.

Harshly he ordered: 'Turn your horses an' start off back to Sacramento. Go on, get movin'.' They turned slowly, reluctantly, so the cattleman pulled trigger and sent lead spanging just over their heads and that quickened their movements.

As they pulled round, preparatory to galloping off down the trail, Jack called: 'If I ever see your dirty, hang-dog faces agen, I'll pull the trigger and that time I won't miss!'

The pair went thundering off down the trail. Iron Jack, contemptuously sardonic, watched their retreat before pulling round and resuming his journey again. He felt that footpads were no account, and he'd lick them every time he met up with them. And the encounter hadn't lost him more than a minute or so of time, so that it didn't amount to anything in his plans.

A moment later, in fact, he had forgotten the incident completely. His thoughts were now concentrated on the blizzard that was blowing up, and the safety of the wagon train high up in the pass before him.

The snow was falling more often now, and the cold was piercing and promised even more snow. Jack Irons, who lived most of his life along the hot, sunny Border, disliked the intense cold and wished himself far away from it. But his life on the range had made him a philosopher — nothing ever lasted, he had learned, not even cold and snow and icy winds. In time he'd have battled his way through them and would be descending to more agreeable temperatures over in Nevada.

He began to be worried when the snow fell so heavily that within the space of half an hour the trail between the mountains was fetlock deep in crisp, crunching whiteness. If this snow kept on, that train might get bogged down and be unable to struggle through the pass for a couple of months or more.

He thought: 'If the pass gets snowed under in winter it won't be any good as a route for the Pony Express.' Then he remembered a lower, more circuitous route, too rough for wagons but good enough for cattle-driving, eight miles south of the trail. It was more sheltered by steep-sided mountains, and it was reported to be always free from snow in winter. That would be the route for the Pony Express when they got into California, on their last lap in their overland race with the mail.

An hour before dusk, early at that time of year, he began to notice the wheel tracks of the train ahead of him. As he rode on they became plainer until he was able to see where the wagon axle-trees had scraped smooth the snow between the high wheels. At this rate it wouldn't be long before the weight of snow became too great to be pushed aside and the wagons would be embedded fast in it.

He sent his horse plunging more quickly in pursuit of the wazons, and because the many wheels had packed the snow into parallel hard paths he made far better pace than the loaded vehicles.

Suddenly he came upon them. He found them digging their way out of a drift where the road levelled somewhat and allowed the snow to gather in a long pocket. He pushed his horse alongside the stationary wagons, with their drooping, soft-lowing pairs of oxen, distressed by their hard day and blowing clouds of steamy breath into the darkening sky. The teamsters, wrapped into shapeless bundles high up on their seats, didn't seem to notice him.

The leading wagon had been got through by the time Jack Irons rode up to them, and a team of spare horses was being hitched to the second span of oxen. About a dozen men were in front, most of them dismounted and holding shovels with which they had been clearing the snow.

As Irons drew rein, the first of a fresh fall of snow began. It drew a curse from one of the mounted men supervising the hitching on of the horses. At that moment he turned and saw Jack Irons.

The cattleman looked into the face of a small, dark-browed man — an unpleasant, overbearing little face . . . the face of a man who is continually in ill-temper with everyone and everything. A bully, and nonetheless to be feared for all his small stature.

Irons thought, instantly: 'Jud Awker.' He'd never met the freight-line operator, but all along the coast Awker's reputation was known, and he recognized him from his description.

He was surprised to see him here with this train, then remembered that he'd heard of Awker's habit of going out as wagon-master with important convoys. He wondered why this twenty-wagon train was important . . .

Jud Awker shouted through the swirling flakes: 'What'n hell do you want, fellar?'

A voice answered — if it was an answer — for Jack Irons. 'This is Iron Jack, Jud. You should watch your tongue in the presence of Mr Irons, for he has a reputation to maintain, I reckon.'

Irons didn't need to turn to look at that other huddled rider to know who owned that mocking voice.

He said, mildly: 'I don't have any reputation to maintain — *Rowlands*.' And that let Rolly Weyte know that he had been recognized.

Jud Awker looked swiftly over in Weyte's direction, however — a quick glance, but to the watchful cattleman it seemed full of complicity. And it also seemed to Irons that the little man was a shade surprised and even taken aback.

Then Awker recovered. 'What're we standin' here for?' he bellowed. 'Get them wagons movin'. We've got to get through the pass before we rest up, otherwise we'll lose the wagons for a coupla months.'

Instantly there was noise and sudden, frantic endeavour. The teamster of the second wagon shouted hoarsely and cracked his whip over the backs of his eight oxen; they lowed dismally and strained against their yokes, while the lead horses reared and plunged their weight forward. The wheels moved, the wagon creaked, and the snow-covered canvas cover swayed to the movement and seemed almost about to fall off. Then the second wagon was through the drift, and the horses were brought back to help with the third vehicle.

Irons pulled round and hitched a rope so that his own horse could lend its strength. Time was running against them; by the sound of it they were near to the top of the pass, but with the snow driving heavily on to the trail it would take them all their time to pull through it.

The wagons began to go through more quickly, now that the first wagons had packed the snow. Irons saw that for the moment they didn't need him, so he sent his willing beast plunging knee deep alongside the trail in search of Ann Caudry.

Instead he ran into Weyte, and it looked as though the mine-owner had deliberately placed himself along the trail so as to intercept any attempt to speak with the girl.

Irons saw a big, hulking figure alongside one of the remaining, stationary wagons. It was now nearly dark and difficult to see, but the cattleman guessed that it was Weyte.

He called: 'That you — Rowlands?'

The mine-owner returned, affably: 'It's me — Weyte.'

'Sure,' agreed Irons, nodding, 'it's you, Rowlands Weyte. But you were just Rowlands back in Kansas, weren't you?'

Rowlands seemed merely amused. 'Me, I've never been in Kansas. But Iron Jack has, I reckon — an' he lit out mighty quick, from all accounts.'

Jack Irons didn't lose his temper, either. 'Sure,' he agreed. 'Wouldn't you have hit the trail, with a posse an' a rope only half a mile down the road after you?' And then he said: 'I reckon you'll have told Miss Caudry about that story, Rowlands.'

Weyte nodded. 'You're right. It was the first thing I did. I told her Kansas State had been plastered with your description a few years back — an' why.' He was laughing at Irons, arrogantly confident in his command of the situation.

Irons still didn't lose his temper. He

was a man who believed in the adage that he who loses his temper loses everything. And often, in the Golden West of those days, the only thing a man had to lose was his life.

He asked, almost mildly: 'Why did you have to tell her?' And Rowlands answered with the most perfect candour.

'Why? Because she was lookin' at you more'n a mite interested, that day you sat together in the Bedrock. Women do get like that about you, don't they, Iron Jack?'

Irons said, gently, 'Don't call me that. It's a silly name to give a fellar.' Then he asked: 'You jealous, Rowlands?'

They were sitting very close together on their horses, the wagon cover by their side pressed into hollows by the weight of the heavily falling snow, so that the supporting hoops showed up like gaunt ribs.

Rowlands peered through the darkness and laughed in derision — yet went on speaking the truth because he couldn't be bothered to lie.

'Not jealous — just careful.' He leaned even closer, so that he didn't have to shout to be heard above the moaning wind that came with the driving snow. 'I've got my mark on that gal. She's mine, d'you hear, Iron Jack? I'm goin' to have her, an' I don't want any fellars like you interferin'.'

The cattleman dug deeper into the collar of his leather coat and bent his head so that his broad-brimmed hat shielded his face from the snow. And his voice was still as gentle as ever as he said, 'I remember one time back in Kansas City when you felt that way about a gal called Belle Storr. Only it didn't last, did it?'

Rowlands never stopped smiling. 'It didn't last,' he said, and his voice was quite cheerful. 'You killed her, so it couldn't last, could it?'

The cattleman sighed, like a man who has been through all this before, many times. 'Were you,' he enquired, 'around when it happened?' And

Rowlands went back to the lie that he had uttered a while ago — a statement that was manifestly untrue, and he knew it but it amused him to repeat it.

'You forget that I told you I've never been in Kansas, Iron Jack!' Then he became over-bold. 'You want to talk to Miss Caudry? OK, she's in the next wagon behind.' He pulled his horse to one side and started to walk it away. 'Guess you won't get much change out of Ann,' he laughed.

The cattleman rode to the rear of the wagon indicated. The cover was strung down at the back, and he knocked against the frozen, board-like canvas until he heard the girl's voice call, 'Hang on, there. Who is it?'

He didn't answer. Instead he looked at the yellow light that came through the canvas where it overlapped poorly, and watched silently while nimble fingers inside tugged on the stiff tie-ropes. A flap came open, and the blonde prettiness of Ann Caudry was revealed in the soft light from a swinging lamp suspended from the arched cover support.

Ann recognized him immediately. Jack Irons was watching her face intently and saw the swift, changing play of emotions across that pretty countenance.

And he was ready to swear that at first sight of him there was, for a fleeting moment of time, a gladness in her eyes. As if she found pleasure in seeing him there, unexpectedly in the snowy wildness of those Nevada mountains.

And then it was gone. Gone, all in an instant. And the cattleman found himself looking into a face that was devoid of emotion, unless it was that it contained fear.

At which moment a loop fell across his shoulders. A weight swung on the rope and he found himself being dragged out of the saddle and over his head in soft, yielding snow.

He saw three mounted figures standing over him, discernible now only as silhouettes against the grey evening sky. And he heard a mocking voice say: 'Didn't I tell you to keep away from Miss Caudry, Iron Jack?'

3

The cattleman saw the fair face of Ann looking down at him from between the parted covers, and there was alarm on it. He tried to struggle into a sitting position and throw off the rope, but each time he rose a jerk pulled him back into the snow again.

He thought: 'That's Rowlands. He's playin' with me.' So he lay still so as not to give the man any satisfaction. He was trying to get to his gun when he heard Jud Awker's bellowing voice: 'What'n hell's goin' on here?'

And then some dismounted man came and hoisted him to his feet. Rowlands said glibly: 'I told Iron Jack to keep away from my charge, Jud. Next thing, I saw him sneaking up to her wagon, tryin' to get in.'

Jack Irons shrugged off the rope and knocked the snow out of his clothes. He said, without any heat: 'That's a downright lie.' But he knew there was no use making more than a formal protest, because no one wanted his opinion, anyway.

Jud Awker shouted: 'I don't give a damn about anythin' except gettin' this train over the pass before it gets blocked. Put that fellar to work on one of the wheels. We'll settle with him when we're down in Nevada.'

Jack Irons saw them lead his horse away, and knew they had him. Now he couldn't leave this convoy, because it would mean death to be alone without a horse in this blizzard.

The man who had hoisted him on to his feet shouted 'Get movin', fellar. The boss says lay on that wheel. Waal, *lay on it!*'

The drift was gathering again on the nearly level stretch of road, so that the remaining wagons were having to be manhandled through. Without any word of protest, Jack Irons put his weight on to a wheel while the lead horses and the team of oxen strained and slowly pulled it through.

It was well past darkness when the last wagon came lumbering up the trail in the wake of the others. They were strung out over a good distance now, and at last word came down the line that the leading wagon was through the gap and descending the Nevada side of the range.

Little Jud Awker, tyrannical boss of the outfit, wouldn't give them any rest. All night he drove them, first to get all the wagons safely through the gap, and then to bring them a safe distance down the lee side of the Nevadas where the storm couldn't do them any harm. That meant that it was dawn before he permitted them to relax.

Only then did he give the word to halt, at a place where a narrow defile sheltered them from the following wind.

Dawn was a grey light ahead of them; Jack Irons was watching it, and making his calculations. He had no intention of remaining in the power of the arrogant, mocking Rolly Weyte, as he seemed to be known in the Golden West, for he had no illusions about the man. He had suspected Rowlands of being behind the hunt that had been set up after him in Kansas — and he thought he knew why. Rowlands might be glad of this meeting, here in the wilderness, and Jack Irons didn't think much to the quality of mercy resident in the wagon-master, Jud Awker.

He had a feeling that the two were pretty close in their companionship, and the expression 'thick as thieves' rose to his lips.

So when Awker came riding past him in the thick carpet of snow, Iron Jack rose from under a wagon, took him by the leg and hurled him clean out of the saddle. Before the boss's cry of warning could take effect, Irons was in the saddle, crouching low and urging the horse into a gallop down the wagon line.

As he came level with the girl's

wagon he leaned over and gave the sagging canvas a hefty clump with his gloved hand. He didn't know why he did it, but it seemed to give him a little satisfaction, though no sound came from the girl within.

The men up front had heard their boss's cry, but at first, when they saw the familiar horse galloping towards them, they thought it was Awker himself riding up. So, as he had hoped, Irons was able to ride past them without any attempt being made to stop him.

He spurred his horse hard once he'd left the last team of oxen behind him, and sure enough a spatter of lead and then the sound of barking revolvers followed him. They did no damage, and then he was away out of sight round a turn in the defile.

He rode down the trail until he was in clear country beyond, and even then he continued until the snow thinned and finally faded and there was nothing to show hoof-prints. Then he turned into a wooded arroyo and dismounted.

It was only then, when he was searching in the saddle-bags for food, that he realized he was in luck. Awker carried a spare .45 in a waterproof pouch. It was a good one, and nearly new, too, so that once again he felt able to face his enemies.

There was no food, so he had to lie up and watch his horse crop the grass that grew sparsely on this poor soil. He had tobacco and papers, however, so that he was able to console himself with plenty of cigarettes.

All day he waited. Rowlands had stated his intentions regarding the girl — he had marked her for his own, and Irons knew what that meant, with a man like the arrogant, insolent mine-owner. Just now he was playing the gentleman, thoughtful, kindly and solicitous. But when it suited him he could be different, much different.

Sitting back there beneath an over-hang of rock, Irons thought: 'It only needs for him to go a bit too fast with the gal.' He had a hunch that the girl liked Rowlands, but she was completely heart-free. Rowlands would tire of playing the gentleman, out here in the wilderness where manners weren't set much store by anyway; he'd show his hand maybe a bit more roughly, and, if the girl repulsed him . . .

'Then she'll see the mean side to Rowlands' character,' he thought.

So he sat there and waited for the wagon train to catch up with him. He had plans regarding Ann Caudry. Part of the plan was dictated by natural thoughts of squaring accounts with the man whom he had always felt to be his enemy, but there were other reasons, too.

Sitting there, not daring to light a fire because he knew they'd see it miles back up the mountain trail, he tried to tell himself he was concerned because Senator Gwin had asked him to look after the girl. But in his heart he knew that was only an excuse.

He was doing too much day-dreaming about the pretty, fair-haired girl from Kansas City for him not to know the real reason behind his planning.

Kansas City . . . When that thought came into his mind he began to wonder again if the girl had lived there during the time that he had been a citizen of the town. He rolled another cigarette thoughtfully. She'd have been a kid of thirteen or fourteen then, he decided. Maybe she wouldn't have heard of the tragedy at the time; wise parents didn't always tell their children of such shocking events.

But she knew now. Probably knew now the worst interpretation of events, because it had come from Rowlands, the one man who had wanted the unfortunate Belle Storr out of the way — because he had tired of her, just as he had tired of other love affairs . . . as he would tire of Ann Caudry, if she was foolish enough to believe his talk of love.

Then he saw the wagon train heaving into view round the shoulder of an abrupt hill. Jud Awker hadn't given his men and beasts much time to recover; a wise wagonmaster, he had known that every foot down that mountain side ultimately meant for greater rest and comfort for his train.

Irons sat back, well screened from the road, and watched while the tired procession approached, drew level, and then passed. Because of the imminence of darkness he knew that the wagon train would not be long before it circled up for the night. Sure enough, less than half a mile along the trail from him, he heard shouts and then the train began the familiar circling preparatory to halting.

He watched while the oxen were unyoked and put out to feed; he saw three big fires flame yellowly within the wagon ring, and watched while men went across to sit by their warmth and eat and drink. It made his hunger pangs more acute, and he knew that he would have to sneak into the camp after dark and get food before he considered any action concerning the girl.

Within an hour the camp was silent. A crescent moon was just rising, giving some light, but he only knew of the situation of the train by the red-glowing embers of the three camp fires.

It seemed to him that two men were left on guard — one circling the draught oxen, while the other kept watch around the wagons.

Leaving his horse, he walked over towards the white-covered prairie schooners, openly, because he knew where the guards were by the glow of their cigarettes. Alongside the first of the wagons he paused, listening. Snores came from within — more snores arose from the wagon next to it. He thought that he had little to fear; the men would be sleeping the sleep of the exhausted, after two days and a night on the hard trail.

A quick survey revealed the chuck wagon, and he climbed in and fumbled around until he felt a sack of beans and then a hunk of meat. The beans weren't any good to him just then, but he lowered it to the ground outside to await his departure, then sat down inside the wagon and got to work on the dried meat. It was tough going, and not to everyone's palate; but a man who lived the trails as Irons did wasn't fastidious. It was food, and he was hungry, so he ate it.

When he'd had enough, he risked striking a match and found some coffee, a pot and a small pan. He also found some parched corn and some welcome tobacco, and, excepting the latter, he put everything into his pack and stole back with it to his horse.

He was now well-equipped, except for water, for the trail ahead. The next part of his plan concerned the girl. He wasn't going to leave her with Rowlands.

This time he rode cautiously up towards the camp. On his first trip he had spotted the place where the horses were picketed, staked by long ropes on a grassy shelf close up against the wagon ring. The guard riding around the wagons had these under his eye, the oxen being herded farther along the valley.

He paused to let the night rider walk his mount slowly away on his round of the wagon train, and then the cattleman touched his heels into his horse's sides and rode quietly in among the picketed beasts.

Without dismounting he bent over and dragged up the stakes that held the picketing ropes. When he had released all the beasts, he leaned over a big bay, that was young and obviously nervous because of its rolling white eyes, and cracked it viciously on the rump.

At once it skittered away from the blow, rearing and plunging, its breath snorting out in a succession of quick sounds that must have carried easily to the ears of the guard across the wagon circle. Then the bay started to run.

That was how Irons wanted it. The frightened young horse knocked into its companions, spreading panic. They rose on their hind-legs, plunging and kicking in their fear and adding to their own sudden terror. Then they found themselves free and started to bolt back up the trail.

The guard came racing around the wagons, shouting. Irons saw him coming and pulled in between two wagons, and the rider went racing by without seeing him. The camp was stirring; men were dropping out from the covered wagons and running across to the scene of the commotion.

He heard Awker's raucous bellow: 'What'n hell's up?' Irons realized that he had picked a good place to hide, for the men were all running away from him, up the trail after the horses.

Then a voice shouted back: 'The hosses has git away, boss. Reckon they was frightened by a mount'n lion.'

Irons listened and a faint smile played over his features as he heard the convenient explanation. That was going to help him. Let them look for a lion as being the cause of the night's disturbance, and not a man, and he might succeed with his plans.

A lamp glowed suddenly from one of the wagons. At once Irons started across towards it. He guessed it would be Ann's. As he came up he heard the girl's voice:

'What's the matter? Has something happened?'

The cattleman tried to disguise his voice as he answered: 'Yeah . . . Better get dressed, ma'am, an' come out.'

She said: 'I am dressed.'

Irons pulled his horse up against the tail of the wagon. 'I'll help you out, ma'am,' he offered politely.

She didn't suspect anything. She must have thought him to be one of the hands sent up by Weyte or Awker, and she leaned out over the tail-board and let Irons lift her across his horse before him.

Some of the men by now seemed to have caught their horses up the valley trail, and that meant it wouldn't be long before the others were rounded up and everyone came back to camp.

He set his horse to a canter down the trail, away from the wagons. He heard Ann's voice ask, very quickly: 'What's happened? Is it — Indians?'

She was very stiff in his arms now, alarmed and disturbed because they were riding away from the wagons. It would only be a matter of seconds before she grew suspicious — and began to be troublesome.

He urged his horse into a gallop, but didn't speak. He heard her say: 'I don't understand. There was no shooting.' And then she panicked, suspecting all was not well with her.

'Where are we going?' Her head was turning. She looked into his face, peering in the wan moonlight. Then she recognized him. He saw her face grow startled, saw fear blossom in her eyes, and it hurt him that she should regard him that way.

'You!' she gasped.

'Me,' he said quickly. 'Jack Irons.' Every second carried them farther away from the wagon train; every second gave greater security to him and his plans.

Urgently he talked to her, trying to keep her from screaming and starting a pursuit.

'Miss Caudry, don't be scared. No harm will come to you. I'm taking you away from Weyte for your own safety.'

But that was too much for her. To be suddenly dragged from her wagon in the middle of the night and ridden away from the security of the wagon train, was more than she could understand. At that moment, in her panic, all she could remember was the story Rolly Weyte had told her about Iron Jack. He was a man for whom a warrant was out in Kansas in connection with the brutal slaying of a girl.

He saw her mouth open to scream. Mentally he sighed. He didn't want to do it, but he wasn't going to have his plans spoilt because the girl took fright at him in the darkness.

His left hand swung across her face, stifling back the scream. She began to struggle in terror at the movement, trying frantically to jerk her head away so that she could shout for help. But he was as tough as only a cattleman can be, and she was as helpless as a child in his strong arms. Though she went on fighting, she found herself unable to tear his hand from across her mouth; and her struggles to throw herself off the horse didn't seem to affect him and served only to tire her within a few minutes. In that time she began to think that Iron Jack was well-named.

He galloped steadily for ten minutes, risking a fall on the poorly lit trail, and then, deciding there was no pursuit as yet, he settled his horse into a walk. Only then did he release his hand from over the girl's mouth.

'Sorry I had to do that, Miss Caudry,' he said politely. 'But it was for your own good. Your uncle sent me after you to take care of you, an' I reckon this is the only way I c'n do it.'

He knew she was trying to shrink away from him, knew she was terrified of him in the darkness. He didn't like it, so he went on talking, trying to reassure the girl and put an end to her fears.

'I'm goin' for your uncle to try to talk Will Russell into startin' a Pony Express. But you know that. He's worried about you comin' overland in the company of Rowlands — Rolly Weyte, that is — an' he asked me to take care of you.'

She found her voice then. 'Is this — taking care of me?'

He sighed, then a note of humour crept into his voice. 'Mebbe it does seem a queer way, Miss Caudry, but — what else could I do?'

She had courage. 'You could have left me with the wagon train. I was safe enough with Mr Weyte and Mr Awker.'

'That,' said Jack Irons gently, 'is where you're mistaken, miss. No gal's safe with Rolly Weyte, I reckon.

She asked, spiritedly: 'What's wrong with Rolly Weyte? You — ' She curbed her impetuous speech suddenly, but the cattleman knew what was in her mind.

'You were goin' to say: 'You haven't much room to talk', weren't you, miss?' His voice was gently chiding, but no more than that. If she had expected rage from him at her unspoken thoughts, she found herself to be mistaken. He didn't seem bothered by them in the least.

'Well, have you?' she demanded, made incautious by anger.

'Mebbe not.' He shrugged. 'But I've never done what I reckon Rolly Weyte did.'

'And that is?'

Irons' voice came softly through the darkness: 'Killed a gal who loved him.'

She became frightened, suddenly. This talk of death while they rode so close together through the dark was unnerving. She found herself whispering: 'Please — please don't let us talk about such things. I — I don't like it.'

She looked round desperately, but there was nothing to see save the ghostly grey shapes of trail-side bushes as they rode beneath a feeble, wintry moon.

'All right, we won't talk at all, then,'

he told her. 'I'll only say again, Miss Caudry, there ain't no harm comin' to you from me — nor from anyone, while I'm around.'

The last words came out suddenly, in a low, threatening growl. They made the girl shiver, and then, unexpectedly, they seemed to give her assurance and comfort, and she slowly relaxed.

By dawn she was asleep in his arms.

Breakfast was made when a red, unwarming sun broke through low cloud in the east. Irons halted when they came to a rivulet that had probably started with the falling snow in the mountains.

He dismounted, then pulled the girl gently down from the horse. She was stiff and heavy with fatigue, so that she fell into his arms without protest or resistance, and he carried her to a patch of soft sand and placed her on it. She watched as he stood over her, her eyes dull and incurious, half-closed in the sleep that she craved. He put his leather coat across her and went and made breakfast. She was fast asleep when he returned with the hot food.

'Sorry, gal, I got to waken you,' he murmured apologetically, and gently shook her into wakefulness. She felt better after the hot food and coffee. She didn't like it without sugar, and made faces, but all the same it went down and seemed to revive her.

Jack Irons squatted on his heels, eating the corn mash and bacon left in the pan. 'Your friends will be hard after us when they know you've been taken away from 'em. That's why I kept goin' all night, and why we've got to keep goin' until I've put you where you'll be safe.'

'Where's that?' She wasn't meeting his eyes this morning, as if she was afraid to see something there that would shake her uneasy trust in him.

'Salt Lake City. I'll fix you on an East-bound coach.'

'Salt Lake City!' Her head jerked up in astonishment. 'Why, that's four or five hundred miles along the trail.'

She didn't say any more, but Irons knew what was going on in her mind. She was viewing with horror the possibility of being alone with him all that way. Alone — and riding between his arms all day!

The cattleman said, gently: 'You don't have to be scared, miss. You won't come to no harm with me, I tell you. An' when we get to Carson City I'll fix you on your own hoss.' He seemed to consider for a moment, as if a new thought had struck him. 'D'you think you could ride a hoss all that way?'

She let her eyes drop. She was thinking — of what could be done in Carson City. 'Yes,' she answered. 'I could ride a horse clean across America, I think. I've ridden horses all my life.'

He rose. His eyes were searching the long, bare trail back up into the mountains. He was thinking, 'If they don't find the gal's missin' until this mornin', that'll have given me a good start ahead of 'em.' But there was always the chance that her abduction had been discovered in the night, when the men returned with their horses, and if so, if Weyte and others had set off in immediate pursuit, they would be close on their heels right now.

He finished breakfast quickly, and packed the spare food away, preparatory to moving off again. The girl was stiff and could hardly rise from the sand, so he bent and helped her up.

She murmured: 'Thank you,' and she looked so pathetically helpless that his sense of kindness was touched again.

'You'll be thinkin' the worst of me, draggin' you away from a comfortable wagon. But it's for your own good, I reckon.' And then, before even riding away from possible pursuit, he decided to take time off to tell her why he had done it.

'He's a friend of yours, miss, that Weyte fellar, but he's bad medicine. I knew him back in Kansas City. He had a gal called Belle Storr, who thought the world of him. One day he learned that she hadn't the money he thought she had, so he said straight out he was finished with her.'

Ann asked: 'How do you know he did?'

'Because Belle told me so, only a little while before she died. She said she was so crazy about him, she wouldn't let it go at that, and she went after him to try'n make him change his mind. That's when I met her, just before she caught up with him, I reckon. I met her on the trail, one hot summer's day, not far from Kansas City. I'd known Belle a long time, and she was a good, quiet gal, livin' with an aunt since her parents died of fever.'

He was lost in the past, the cold of this morning dissipated by the memory of that scorching afternoon on the prairie. His eyes were narrowed and far away. Then he heard Ann's voice.

'Belle Storr — was that the girl you . . . killed?'

He dragged his eyes round to her. They were patient, not hurt or angry. 'I didn't kill her. I've never killed anyone, not like that. Don't you see, Ann, I couldn't be talkin' about it if I had.'

Ann. Not miss or ma'am this time. She noticed it, but didn't comment upon the familiarity. Instead she asked, hesitantly: 'Were you in love with Belle?'

'Me? In love with Belle?' The question surprised him. 'No — no, miss, I never loved any gal, I reckon.' Then his eyes came back to her blue ones, as if to test the truth of his statement, and when they went away there was doubt in them.

'Who killed her, then?'

Irons spread out his gloved hands. 'I don't know. Nobody knows. Not many minutes after she'd left me she was found murdered along the trail. They saw me riding away — someone had even seen me talkin' with her almost at the place where her body was found. So they got down to thinkin' I'd done it, I reckon.' He shrugged cynically. 'First thing they did was to put a noose on a rope. Then they tried to put me inside that noose. So I pulled a gun an' got away from 'em an' never stopped till I was in Texas. That was a foreign country in them days.'

'You never went back to clear your name?'

'Ma'am,' Irons said politely, 'when a crowd of fellars is waitin' to talk justice with a rope already noosed you keep right away from 'em — if you've sense. Wal, I had sense, I guess. My name was bad in Kansas, but I was alive on the Border. It was good enough.'

He stooped suddenly and picked her up and sat her in front of his saddle. He had spent enough time in talking. He climbed up behind her and pushed his horse into an easy trot.

But the girl was still curious, still had questions to ask him.

'Why do you think Weyte had anything to do with the girl's death?'

Irons looked across the broken, desolate landscape and considered. 'It was just things he said. Belle had told me he'd jilted her. When I shouted this out to that posse with the rope, Weyte stood up and shouted back it was a lie. He said Belle was his gal, an' he'd intended to marry her, an' he'd never jilted her at all. Then he got to encouragin' the posse to use that rope.'

'That's all you have against him?'

'It's a lot, ain't it? A fellar doesn't lie unless he's got good reason. I figger Weyte's reason was because he'd killed the gal an' hoped to fix the blame on me.'

'You think they met when Belle left you, and he killed her . . . because she had become an embarrassment to him?'

'I figger he was back there along the trail, watchin' us all the time. I figger Belle's followin' him was upsettin' his plans. Maybe they talked. Maybe they quarrelled. Maybe he lost his temper and did it. Maybe.'

She brought her head round at that, questioning the note in his voice.

'I think,' he said harshly, 'maybe he deliberately killed her in cold blood with the idea of fixin' the thing on me. Rowlands — that's the name I knew him by in Kansas City — isn't the kind of man to lose his temper, an' when he does things he does 'em for a purpose.'

He felt the girl shiver in his arms, but the grating mood didn't immediately leave him.

'I figger the fellar's mad,' he went on. 'No man could be sane an' do the things that fellar does.'

'You've heard more about him — since?'

'Yeah. Stories — that's all they amount to. But they don't add up to anythin' nice about Rowlands.'

Iron Jack sighed. He didn't know why he should go on, he'd never spoken to anyone about this in all the time he'd been away from Kansas. But having got so far he felt impelled to complete the story for the girl. He found that he badly wanted to have her sympathy, yet bitterly he wondered why he should try — every man always tried to excuse himself, and she wouldn't believe the story he had to tell.

'All the time I was on the Border I kept hearin' drifts of talk about Rowlands. And always his name was connected with women. Even before Kansas City, he hadn't behaved right by the women who were beginning to love him. Looks like Rowlands promised a lot of gals marriage, got his hands on whatever they owned, and then vamoosed. Now he doesn't need to do that any more. Some gal somewhere grubstaked him to California, an' he struck lucky an' now he doesn't need to make love for money.'

They jogged along the bleak, cold trail for a while in silence after that, and then the girl spoke.

'Rolly Weyte's been making up to me.'

Iron Jack looked down upon the fair curls and his face softened. 'Is that to be wondered at?' he asked.

For the first time the girl laughed. 'Why, Mr Irons, I think you meant that as a compliment!'

He merely inclined his head, but didn't add to his statement. Instead he said: 'When Rowlands sees a pretty gal, he puts his mark on her.'

'Puts his mark — ?'

'Marks her out for his own. An' he's the kind of man who goes all out for what he wants, and the more that people try to stop him, the more determined he becomes in tryin' to get what he wants. Like Belle. Poor Belle. He got so that he didn't want her, an' when she began to follow him around he just made sure she wouldn't interfere with his plans. And your uncle doesn't like Rowlands, does he?'

'He doesn't like Rolly Weyte,' admitted Ann. 'He's always mistrusted him and tried to keep him away from me.'

'Your uncle has sense,' said Irons. 'He knows a mean critter when he sees one. But your uncle's attempts to keep Rowlands away only made him the more determined to win you.'

Ann shuddered. Then her hand rose helplessly to brush back a stray curl, and it was trembling. 'I — I just don't know what to believe,' he heard her whisper. Then, minutes later, she asked a final question. 'If you think Weyte killed his old sweetheart, why, when you met him in California, didn't you do something about it? I mean, attack him, or accuse him?'

'I knew Weyte very little in Kansas. He didn't stay long in any place, I reckon. And in those days he had a rough beard. I wasn't sure of him in the Bedrock, at first.'

'But when you were sure?'

'What could I do? After all, I've only suspicion about the man, just as that posse had suspicion about me.'

And more than anything that statement won for him the trust of this girl who rode between his arms. She felt that a man, accused of murder, to be so cautious in passing on the accusation, even where he suspected it should lie, was more than an ordinary man. She seemed to relax after that, as if she had lost a lot of her fear of him.

By noon, Jack Irons was beginning to be apprehensive, and the girl noticed how often he turned to look back at that mighty range of snow-capped mountains. Burdened as his horse was, he knew that fleet and avenging pursuit must soon catch up with them, and he was anxious now to reach Carson City, where he could get a horse for the girl.

Coming down into the town, along the steep rough trail that had been worn by the passage of tens of thousands of gold-mad prospectors, Irons looked back once again — and remained staring intently back for some time. At last the girl asked: 'Are they coming?'

She was surprised to find that in some way she shared his apprehension, as if she didn't want the pursuit to catch up with them, and it made her a little angry. Of course she wanted help to ride up, she told herself; she couldn't go on trusting herself to a man whose name, by all accounts, was synonymous with brutal murder all over the State of

Kansas. True, he had spoken convincingly — had even made her believe in him — but the fact remained that she had only his word for the story he told . . . and what did that amount to?

He turned to look down into the town, in the valley below. His voice was soft as he answered: 'There's men ridin' hard behind us. Looks like three of 'em. Mebbe it's Rowlands tryin' to get you back from me.'

Then he added, with certainty in his voice: 'He'll try to kill me for takin' you. It will also be a good excuse to quieten me.'

Her head jerked round, so that her wide, frightened eyes looked at him. 'He'll try . . . to kill you?' She forgot her recent attempt to be angry with him, forgot the doubts she had deliberately raised in her own mind against his story. At the prospect of his being killed she found that she didn't really dislike the man as much as she pretended.

'Sure.' He urged his horse faster, now that his goal was in sight. 'You don't know a fellar like Rowlands. He's dead set on gettin' you, and he's the kind to ride through hell an' high water to get what he's after. He'll want to kill me for tryin' to steal you away from him.'

Just outside Carson City they came to a rude tavern at the trailside. Irons pulled in, calling to a bearded man attending to some horses under a lean-to: 'You got any hosses I c'n buy, pardner?'

The man straightened, then came slowly out. His eyes went appreciatively over Jud Awker's fine, if tired, mount. 'You want to trade that for one?'

Irons nodded, dismounting and helping the girl down. 'Yeah. And I want a hoss for this lady, too.' He pulled out some Mexican silver dollars to show he meant business. Time was urgent. In less than five minutes the pursuers would be upon them.

The tavern proprietor wanted to haggle, but Irons cut him short by making an outright bid for two good young horses under the lean-to. The price was good enough to make the bearded man close immediately, in case the prospective buyer thought twice and withdrew the bid.

Irons helped to saddle up, then went across to lift the girl on to her horse. She had walked away towards the front of the log cabin, where a knot of men were standing looking through the open door at them.

As Irons came up, leading her horse, she said, quickly, but quiet enough so that the loungers at the bar couldn't hear her words: 'I'm not coming on with you. You'd better go by yourself.'

Irons stood stock still, trying to think around this unexpected situation. Then he began to say: 'Ann — Miss Ann, you mustn't stay here. I tell you, you'll want to kill yourself if you fall into Rowlands' hands. He'll treat you bad, because that's the only way that critter knows how to treat a woman. He's crazy, I tell you.'

'I'm not going with Rowlands, either.' Her eyes came back to his for a second. 'I — I don't know what to think about you, or about Rolly Weyte. I — I just feel it would be better — safer — for me not to trust myself to either of you.'

He looked back up the trail. For the moment there was no one in sight. 'Ann,' he begged, 'trust me as far as Virginia City at least, then you won't be bothered by Rowlands.'

He was frantic at the thought of this girl falling into Rowlands' hands again. His hand reached out to take her by the shoulder and pull her round to see him. She started to struggle, and tried to pull herself away. Irons heard the rapid advance of hoofs in the distance; turned and saw three riders careering down the trail only a couple of hundred yards away.

'He won't let you stay here,' he shouted. 'Don't be a fool, Ann. He'll force you to go with him!'

In his urgency he took hold of the girl and tried to lift her into the saddle, but the action only threw her into alarm, and she struggled and cried out.

At once men began to flood out of the log tavern, shouting angrily at this man who assaulted a girl before their eyes. Irons tried to hold the frantic girl, failed, and spun round to meet the charge of the miners. They were brutal in their methods. They came in with their heavy, ironshod boots kicking, their powerful hairy fists pounding.

Irons went down before the rush. He hit the hard, bare ground, and his body seemed to erupt with pain as their boots drove into him. There was dust in his nostrils, feet stamping around his head, men bawling hoarsely as they strove to avenge this insult to a lady.

He tried to roll away, but there was no escape, and within seconds he would have been kicked out of consciousness, only there came an interruption. Dazed, he felt a weight suddenly flung on top of him — there was a body shielding his own from those savage blows. It was Ann, protecting him.

He realized that the kicking had

stopped, felt himself being dragged into a sitting position by the girl. She was crying: 'Don't hurt him! Let him go. He didn't mean to harm me!' Those hooves were thunderously close now.

He was dazed by the sudden, overwhelming assault, and didn't know what to do. Then he felt the girl's frantic hands pulling on his leather coat, dragging him to his feet. He wiped the blood from his eyes, where it flowed from a long nail mark across his forehead. Saw Ann's pretty face, now filled with concern, staring in horror at his own bloody mask. Then she began to shove him across to his horse.

'Leave me,' she was urging. 'Get away from Rowlands. If he lays hold of you he'll ... ' She didn't finish her sentence.

The rough, bearded miners were hanging back, not sure what to make of it all. Ann got the cattleman across to his horse and helped him to swing into the saddle. Someone ripped off with a Colt, making the horse rear and almost throw off the still-dazed rider. Ann turned, saw Rolly Weyte racing up within fifty yards of them — behind were two scrub-faced ruffians, whom she remembered seeing at the beginning of the trek from San Francisco.

Weyte had his gun out. He raised it to fire again. Ann lost any feeling she ever had for Weyte at sight of that gesture; for the mine-owner had his mouth open as if in enjoyment at the prospect of killing.

Ann drove her fist into the soft belly of Irons' young horse. It wasn't the sort of thing a young lady normally did, but she'd seen men do it, and now in an emergency she did it instinctively.

It made the horse leap forward, causing Weyte to miss with that second bullet, and then the miners scattered as it went charging down into Carson City, Irons somehow managing to hang on to his crazy mount.

Weyte swung his horse round, gun raised as he came up in savage pursuit. Then Ann ran right across in front of the saliva-lathered beast, causing its rider to shout in alarm and drag his mount's head around. Before Weyte could stop his horse, it had crashed into one of the supporting poles of the lean-to, bringing the flimsy roof down on three ponies underneath.

For a few seconds the tavern yard was a mad whirl of frightened, kicking horses and shouting men racing up to try to catch them and quieten them. Ann stood back, her face white, her hands pressed against her chest. She saw the man she knew as Rolly Weyte stagger out, then straighten and begin to smile as he always did, no matter the circumstances.

Then he started to walk across towards her, reeling a little as if not recovered from the blow that the falling roof had given his head. Smiling. And talking. Talking to her, and to anyone who was standing around and able to hear him.

And long before his hands took hold of her, Ann Caudry knew that he had beaten her . . . knew that she would have to go with the man, because he was too clever for her.

And she knew, too, that what Iron Jack had told her about the man's character was right — even to the touch of madness that was within him.

4

Irons rode through sprawling, noisy Carson City, scarcely able to hold on to his horse because of the pain in his side where a boot had crashed into his ribs. Fortunately his head was clearing, so that at least he could use his wits as he went thundering along the twisting main street, between canvas-roofed, false-fronted saloons, gambling joints and stores.

He didn't stop, though he needed supplies for the trail and several blankets if he were to sleep out. Rowlands was gunning for him, was not far behind, and Irons was in no condition to face up to the man at the moment.

Once out through the town he struck south-west away from the river, following the direct route to Salt Lake City through the silver town of Virginia City.

Here he settled down to a walk, to ease the pain in his bruised body, and to keep his horse in best condition. Rowlands and his followers weren't in sight, and there was no use in racing along if the pursuit had given up.

He found an isolated store about five miles along the trail where he was able to buy the supplies he needed. The old man who kept the place looked curiously at his battered features, and commented aloud at the stooped way he held himself to relieve the pain in his ribs.

'You been gettin' into trouble, pardner? Them Silver fellars been on to you?'

Irons sat on a nail keg just within the door. He felt numb with pain and cold, but he didn't let on to the storekeeper how badly he felt. Jack Irons believed it no bad thing to hide a weakness from a potential enemy; and in this wild West, any man, even this grizzled old storekeeper, could turn out to be a foe. The fellow had mean eyes, and he did too much looking with them, the cattleman decided.

'I had a fall, back along the trail,' he said, truthfully enough. 'Kinda shook me a bit, but I'll be all right.' Then he asked: 'Who's the Silver fellars?'

'The Silver Gang?' The old man spat. 'Don't know, an' I wouldn't tell ef I did. They're a passel o' *hombres* who ride the trails aroun' Virginie City, stickin' wagons up an' kinda gettin' in everyone's hair.'

Irons looked moodily at the tobacco-stained dirt floor, and thought: 'How's the Pony Express goin' to ride through Virginia City with *hombres* like that watchin' the roads?' For the mails would be a sure target for highway robbers.

At length, rested, he stirred and went out to his horse. The old storekeeper came to the door after him to watch him go, and on an impulse Irons threw him a Mexican dollar, saying: 'If anyone asks after me, try'n forget I ever went by along this trail.'

The old man grabbed the coin with dirty, black-nailed fingers, and said with eager cordiality: 'I sure will, pardner. You trust me. I got a mouth that sure can stay shut when I want it to.'

Irons nodded. He thought that it was money wasted, but just in case Rowlands did ride along or send others after him, it was worth a dollar to try to slip the pursuit.

He rode slowly along the trail, more and more stooped with the pain of his side. His head began to throb again with the constant jolting, and in time he realized that those rough miners, dashing to the rescue of the blue-eyed girl, had hurt him more severely than he'd thought.

He sighed, tried to straighten, and thought: 'Well, at least Ann isn't ridin' with Rowlands any more, even if she's not ridin' with me.' That was some consolation; even the pain he was suffering now was worthwhile if it had saved the girl from the power of the evil Rowlands . . .

The sun came from behind clouds, cold but dazzling to his eyes. The landscape was wild, barren, chilly and depressing, and it seemed to swim before his hot, fevered eyes as if in a heat haze. Only he wasn't hot; he was shivering now in the steady-driving cold wind that drove across this mountainous plateau.

His thoughts began to ramble, and only by instinct did he cling to the saddle. Yet he rode on alone on that winding, wheel-scarred trail.

Alone. But an Indian rode by his side.

Irons saw him once when he lifted his leaden head for a moment. Then his head drooped and his thoughts went rambling crazily to days on the Mexican Border — days of almost unendurable heat, and fighting that was a succession of swift, savage raids upon others, and then fierce, vicious attacks upon themselves . . .

There were two Indians riding silently beside him, one on either side,

110

Indians clad in buffalo robes to meet the winter blast.

But he was back along the Border, fighting with Texans to drive the rapacious tax-collecting Mexicans out so that they could make this vast country theirs ... He was riding again with Bronco Evans, Long-shot Goodry, who could hit a man and knock him off his horse at quarter of a mile with an old Henry muzzle-loader; he was fighting alongside Reuben Raisen, whose life he had saved; Stiffneck Olluss and others. He thought: 'They're the fellars to ride this Pony Express. Silver Gangs wouldn't stop 'em.'

His aching head reared back so that he could look again from under flaming hot lids.

And there were more Indians alongside him now. Many more.

'Not real Injuns,' he said, as his head flopped again and he sprawled across the horse's neck. No, these weren't the wild, untamed Nevada Indians who were such a menace to the white man in spring and summer, when their ponies were fat with the rich new grass, and their own bellies were filled with easily hunted game. These were Indians who had lived with the white man and had learned the worser habits of the invaders of their territory — they were renegades from their tribes, recognizable because most affected white man's dress and carried the white man's weapons.

He tried again to look at them, and succeeded only when he twisted his head and didn't try to lift it as before. They were riding close all around him, looking into his face with cold, unemotional stares. A momentary return out of his rambling state let him see them — and let him see himself, too, at the same time.

He thought: 'Iron Jack — that ain't no name for me right now!' And then he slipped back into his fevered state again.

An Indian rode forward and tipped him out of the saddle. His horse shied away but was instantly caught. Jack Irons crashed on to the rocky ground, and the pain drove him farther into unconsciousness. Just before he passed out completely he had a feeling of ungentle hands pulling open his clothes and going through his pockets.

A long time afterwards, very stiff and cold, he came to consciousness again. He raised himself painfully on his hands and let his weary, pain-laden eyes look around. There was no one in sight. Those Indians had gone off with his horse, leaving him to die on the trail.

He at length succeeded in getting on to his feet, but his staggering legs collapsed after a dozen paces and the shock of the fall nearly sent him unconscious again. He lay there for a while, trying to recover and get his strength back, and when he had succeeded, once more he rose and swayed off in the direction of Virginia City.

He was saying to himself all the while: 'If I lie here I die. I've got to make it — got to walk on till I find help.'

And he drove himself to walk, though his whole frame shrieked a protest at the demands he made upon it, hurt as it was. He walked a good fifty yards this time before collapsing, and this time when he went down he hit his already injured head and stayed down.

He lay there, rambling again. He lay in a world of hot pain, though his body shivered from the bite of the wind that followed him from the snowy Sierras. And more and more his thoughts went to Ann Caudry, so that in his delirium he spoke her name. After a time he could even see her — saw her face, tender and smiling, saw blue eyes that were filled with laughter yet kindly at all times. Saw her as he had seen her in his arms all along that trail into Carson City.

He spoke to her, then listened for her voice, but though she was there she didn't speak back to him. Still, it was comforting to be able to see her, to know that she was near to him, even though she would only smile at him and not speak.

A momentary return to consciousness revealed a blank trail all around him. He stirred wearily. He must be in a bad way for him to have imagined that Ann Caudry had caught up with him and was looking after him, he thought. Then he began to slip back into rambling semi-consciousness again, and he found that he welcomed it — he wanted to be with the girl even if only within his own mind . . .

* * *

He knew he was in a very bad way when Ann started to talk to him, so he took no notice of what she was saying and luxuriated only in the sound of her voice.

Then she started to cry, and he knew there was something wrong then; because he had never known Ann to cry before and so he couldn't see how he was able to picture her weeping now.

Yet she seemed to be there, weeping.

He also thought she was trying to pull him to his feet, and she was watching back along the trail in terror. She was calling to him through her tears, begging him to try to help himself — wanting him to stand and then walk over to her horse and mount it.

And somehow he was in the saddle, lying across the horse's neck . . . Ann was striding out down the trail, leading the horse, watching to see that he didn't fall off, and then watching in fear and dread back along the trail behind them . . .

*   *   *

He was in a cart or a small wagon. He could see the canvas hood swaying above him, could hear the familiar creak-creak of the body as it gave under the bumping, unsprung wheels. He got the familiar smell of sweating horseflesh and heard the clop-clop of unshod hooves on the hard trail . . . And then he saw Ann Caudry.

She was on the driver's seat, reins in hands; she was peering anxiously down at him, where he lay on what seemed to be a thick pile of brushwood.

Then the picture faded.

The next thing he remembered, the canvas cover was red as if it were on fire. He was too weak to do anything for a long time except stare up at the dancing light, and in that time he realized that the wagon was not on fire but that he saw the reflection of a camp fire somewhere in the night outside.

He felt cooler in his head, stiff and sore beyond description, but in some way better. Slowly, painfully, he turned so that he could look out over the tail of the wagon. The tail-board had been dropped, so that by lifting his head only an inch or so he was able to see outside.

Ann was sitting close to a small fire, cooking food in a pan. As he looked she appeared suddenly frightened and halted in her work to peer into the blackness of the night. He saw her hand go out to a revolver which lay at her side, and he guessed it to be the one he had found in Jud Awker's saddle-bag.

He thought she looked lovely, yet strained and tired and on the edge of her nerves.

The cattleman whispered: 'Ann.'

For a moment her wild, startled eyes leapt to the blackness about her, and the gun came up in her hand. He saw her mouth open in fear, yet there was courage in the girl so that she stood up to meet it. Then she realized who it was who had spoken. He saw her come springing quickly across from the fire towards him, and now her face lit up. He found himself looking into her shining eyes as she stood against the tail of the wagon, and he heard her whisper brokenly: 'Oh, thank God, thank God you're getting better! I kept thinking . . .'

She turned her head, so that he couldn't see her tears, but her joy was so great that she couldn't keep her eyes away from him and now she looked back at him and didn't care if he did see her weeping. They were tears of happiness, anyway.

She got into the wagon and fussed over him, making him more comfortable and talking to him all the while. Irons was so far recovered now that he was able to observe the quickness of her speech, the note of hysteria that crept into it; and he didn't want to see her like this, so afraid, so he reached out and took her hand in his and said: 'You don't have to worry any more, Ann. I'll be all right by mornin'. I'll look after you from now on.'

At that she broke down. She sat cross-legged alongside him — he noticed now that she had discarded her feminine attire and wore men's trousers that were too big for her — and she talked as she wept into her hands.

It was a story of two days and three nights on the trail — two days and three nights of sheer terror to the lonely girl, of anguish of mind such as she had never known.

'I couldn't leave you anywhere,' she wept. 'Weyte — Rowlands — is after you and will kill you if he finds you. He's looking for you, Jack, and he means murder.'

'Where'd you get the wagon?' He was astonished to find how weak his voice had become during his illness.

'I bought it from a farmer who hadn't any more use for it. He gave it me for next to nothing when I told him I wanted to get you to a doctor in Virginia City.' She didn't tell him that she had called him her husband so as to enlist the farmer's sympathy. She didn't feel it was necessary.

'I brought you through Virginia City. I didn't dare stop in case Weyte — Rowlands — caught up with us.' She shuddered, and her tears came faster. Now that he was getting better she seemed to be completely unnerved. 'I was terrified. Every time I saw a horseman I thought it was Weyte coming to kill you as you lay helpless. And you — ' Her eyes lifted and he was shocked to see the horror in them. 'You were raving, Jack. You were off your head. I thought any time I'd come to look at you I'd find you . . . dead. I don't know what I'd have done if I'd found you were dead.'

She went across for some food, but it was more to give herself a chance to recover than because she needed something to eat. Irons couldn't eat, but he was glad of some hot, sweet coffee. It did the girl a lot of good, too, and now she stayed with him in the wagon and seemed to find comfort in his company, even though he was still as helpless as he'd been these last two and a half days.

They weren't far from Virginia City. Having come through that wild town of silver miners she had turned off into the wastes and had camped this last day or so well out of sight of the trail.

'You were so ill, I knew you'd have died if I'd kept going down the trail.'

He lay there, relaxing, feeling the strength creep back into his muscles

121

with every passing second. 'You don't need to worry any more,' he told her again. 'I'll soon be around to look after you.' And then he asked: 'What happened at that tavern when you met Rowlands?'

He saw the shudder that ran through the girl, remembering it.

'Rolly Weyte ran into a shed and got thrown off his horse,' she said, but she didn't say that it was her own intervention that had caused the accident. 'That stopped him from following you. I watched you ride off, swaying in the saddle, Jack, and I thought you'd never be able to hold on. I knew those miners had hurt you very severely.'

He murmured: 'Don't blame them, Ann. They thought they were protecting you. And weren't they?'

He liked to see her, sitting over him, her face illuminated by the dancing firelight, her shadow long and black on the red-lit canvas over them.

She was telling him about Rolly Weyte. How he'd come across to her, swaying from the effects of the blow on his head, and yet smiling.

'He was saying, 'That fellar's a hoss thief. He got away with Jud Awker's own hoss, as these fellars'll tell you. An' he ran of with this gal that I'm supposed to take to Virginia City'.'

She sat very still now, her mind back on that moment.

'I knew, the way he said it — the way he got all those men immediately against you for a horse-thief — that I'd never get away from Weyte. It would have been no use appealing to those men for aid, not with him posing as my guardian.'

'So?' he prompted.

'I played double. I didn't say anything about not intending to trust myself with him. Instead I pretended to be very meek and obedient and even glad to see him. But, Jack, I hated having to do it; I was terrified of the man.'

'You realized . . . that what I said about him was right?' Now, when he saw her shudder, he reached out and took her hand.

'Yes.' She looked out at the fire that was slowly dying. 'I think I did. I felt that he was crazy, just as you said.' It was that revealing glimpse of him, in the act of shooting down a helpless man, that had betrayed the madness that Jack Irons had long suspected.

Rolly Weyte had decided against pursuing Irons there and then, though he swore he'd settle with him for abducting the girl, even if he had to follow him right back into Kansas. He'd decided to wait at the tavern until Jud Awker and the freight train pulled in that night; he wanted to make sure that Ann was safe with his friends before taking up Iron Jack's trail, he said.

They found a room for the girl at the back of the tavern. Because her new antipathy to Weyte wasn't suspected, no attempt was made to watch her or lock her up, and the mine-owner and his two companions went in to drink with the miners at the bar.

The girl had found some men's clothes inside the room, and she had started to change into a costume more suitable for the trail than womanly skirts. She had only just completed the change when she heard someone try the door. She didn't stay. She went out the back way, through a door that led to the yard where the horses were; she picked out the horse that Irons had bought for her — it was still saddled and bridled — and she rode off at a gallop.

'I rode back towards Carson City for a while,' she explained, 'to throw them off the trail, then I cut round down by the river until I'd circled the town and got onto the Virginia City trail. Then I found you.'

Irons said: 'I just seem to remember it. I thought I was delirious. But I remember you cried.'

'I cried,' whispered the girl. 'You looked so — helpless. And all the time I was terrified that Rolly Weyte would find you.'

She thought he had been thrown

from his horse, but he told her of those other visitors to his delirium — those city-wise Indians, ever ready to fall upon a defenceless traveller and rob him.

His eyes were drooping and heavy, and there was a content stealing over him that he had never known in his life before.

He heard his own voice, very drowsy. 'What did I say, in my ravin', Ann?'

Her glance came up and met his own; there was mischief and humour mixed with the faintest of embarrassment.

'Oh, about everything and everyone, it seemed. You talked a lot about the war with Mexico. You didn't seem to like it.'

'There were a lot of us didn't like that war,' he answered. 'Too many innocent people got killed . . . women an' children. An' we were as bad as the Mexicans — or worse.'

She averted her head modestly. 'You talked, though, mostly about one person. All the time, it seemed, you talked about that one person.'

His eyes came wide open, staring questioningly up at her as she rose to attend to the fire. 'Who . . . was it?'

'Me,' she told him, jumping down. 'You never stopped talking about me.'

'I'm sorry,' he began, and then she lost her embarrassment, and turned and laughed into his face over the tail of the wagon.

'That's all right, Jack. What you said was most complimentary.' She patted his shoulder reassuringly. 'In fact, I've never heard so many nice things said about me in such a short time.'

She laughed, and it seemed to the sore and injured man that there was happiness in her voice. She was turning away when he called her back.

'Ann,' he told her, his eyes unwavering on her own, 'I don't know what I said, but I know I meant every word of it.' And then he added: 'And, Ann, I'm goin' to be better by the morning. I'm not goin' to have you scared of bein' alone any more.' He, too, had a sense of humour, and now he lifted his head and grinned. 'I never did like the name before, but from now on I am goin' to be Iron Jack. You see if I'm not.'

She laughed, patted him again and went to the fire. When she returned he was asleep. She crept in beside him for warmth out of the cold night wind, and that night she slept for the first time in three days.

The rich aroma of coffee steaming under his nose brought him back to wakefulness. Ann was kneeling over him. She was smiling, and this morning the sun seemed to have warmth and made her face glow healthily pink.

'Feeling better?'

He struggled into a sitting position and she helped him. 'Great,' he told her. He saw the gun stuck into her belt. 'You can leave that off now, Ann. I'll make gun-talk if it's required.'

He felt clear in his mind again, and his voice sounded strong, as he'd always known it. But his muscles were still weak, and the soreness hadn't left him.

She sat with him inside the wagon, and they shared breakfast out of the same pan and drank coffee from the one pot. He admired the way this girl, brought up to a comfortable way of life, fell without complaint into the rude way of living that trail-people knew so well. She was the kind of girl, he thought, to make a good wife for a backwoodsman.

As they breakfasted they talked. Ann was anxious to hit the trail again. 'I want to get back to Kansas City,' she told him, her voice beginning to tremble a little. 'I want to know what's happened to mother. I only hope I'm not too late.'

Irons told her: 'We won't waste another hour. You get finished with the breakfast while I go an' fix the hosses in the traces.'

But when he tried to stand up he found he just hadn't the strength, and he had to suffer the humiliation of lying in the wagon while a girl did all the work. Yet it had to be endured, and within an hour they were creaking along towards the Salt Lake City trail.

That night Irons was so far recovered in strength that he was able to clamber out of the wagon and sit beside the fire while the girl cooked supper. She liked that; she felt safe from the lurking, watching shapes who, in her imagination, peopled the silent wastes beyond the light of the fire. Night-time had been the greatest terror to her when Iron Jack was in delirium and unable to help her. Now he sat with his Colt on his knee, keeping watch while the glowing fire betrayed their presence on the trail. Next morning he felt better. He was awake first and had started the fire before Ann stirred and came out to him.

Three days later they entered Austin, half-way on their journey to Salt Lake City . . . and still the better part of two thousand miles from their goal.

Coming into Austin, Ann gave way to despair at the thought of that immense journey still before them. 'Oh, Jack,' she wept. 'It seems too far; we'll never do it.'

He told her that people were doing it every day. 'Why, you came across America yourself when you came out to your uncle.'

'Not this way. This is so slow. I came by way of Santa Fe, on stage-coaches that did the journey in a few weeks.'

'All right,' he said. 'We'll sell the wagon in Austin, an' we'll buy hosses an' ride fast, instead.'

'But — ' she began to protest.

'All right,' he said, anticipating her remark. 'You don't have to worry. I'm Iron Jack again; an' I reckon to ride as far as you any day. That's how well I am!'

So it was arranged that they should ride fast to Salt Lake City, where Ann would pick up one of the Russell, Majors and Waddell stage-coaches, which gave a fast and frequent service to the East. Irons would travel alone on horseback. He wasn't made for stage-coaching, he

131

said, and besides he, too, was in a hurry to get to Kansas. That Pony Express idea had burned into his brain, and he was impatient to see it in operation.

Mention of Kansas brought a frown to Ann's face. 'Jack,' she asked, looking up at him as he drove towards the town, which sat on the edge of a river that ended in the loose sand of the Nevada desert, 'aren't you scared of being recognized back in Kansas?'

'I'll take the chance,' he said, casually. 'I'm goin' to Leavenworth, about thirty miles north of Kansas City. I don't reckon there'll be anyone there to spot me an' tip me off to a law-man. It's a few years since I was East, an' I reckon the population's changed twice over since I was in Kansas.' But he didn't say that he also intended to visit Kansas City.

She sat by his side, and he felt that she was worrying about him. He said, soothingly: 'You don't need to bother, Ann.' But she shook her fair head, and the face that turned to his was troubled.

'Why do you have to go back?' she asked him. 'It's so dangerous. Your life's at stake, you know.'

'There's someone I've got to see. No, not Russell, though I'm dead keen on givin' him your uncle's message. The more I think of it, the more sure I am that Will Russell will take up this Pony Express idea. But — ' He shrugged. 'There's someone else I must see. I've just got to go, so leave it at that, Ann.'

They were right in Austin, Nevada, when he asked a question that surprised them both. 'You don't want to see me get hurt, Ann. That's a change from one time back on the trail,' he smiled. 'Why have you changed?'

'Rolly Weyte painted you with a black character, Jack — '

'Just as I brushed tar on his,' he countered.

'But you've had the chance to harm me if that was your intention, Iron Jack,' she smiled. 'You've — well, you've been a gentleman all the time, haven't you? Besides — '

'Go on.'

'Well, when you were delirious you went over and over again through that meeting with poor Belle Storr before she went on to meet Rowlands. You were begging her not to have anything to do with him. She — she was going to have a child, wasn't she? And you even offered to marry her and bring up the child as your own.'

Iron Jack's jaw was set as he gazed grimly down the main street that led to the ford. 'I didn't know you knew so much about me.' She heard his voice, harsh and unmusical.

'No?' Ann's voice was very soft. She turned to look at the slow-moving river that ran out into the wastes. 'But I knew from what you said that the story you told me was correct. You watched poor Belle go obstinately after the man she loved, and you turned and went away then, didn't you? The next thing some men were riding after you, shouting at you. One of them was this man you hardly knew — Rowlands,

Belle Storr's lover. He was shouting to the men to catch you and string you up for killing Belle.'

Jack Irons sighed and let his head droop. 'Belle told me her secret. I was the only one that knew, apart from Rowlands. I never thought to let her poor secret pass my lips.'

And then he pulled into a livery stable and dismounted. They spent sparingly, because the only money they possessed was what Ann had had on her in a money belt the night that Iron Jack had ridden away with her. But they indulged in the luxury of a good meal in the inevitable Chinese dining-room, even though they cut provisions for the next part of their journey down to a minimum.

The wagon didn't bring much and they had to be content with inferior mounts, though they were better than the wagon pair that Ann had purchased back near Virginia City. Ann watched while the cattleman bargained shrewdly for new mounts, and the thought in her mind was: 'He told me the truth except in one thing — he lied when he said that he didn't love Belle Storr. He must have done, to have offered to help her as he did.'

It left her with a curious little ache in her heart, as if she didn't want to think of this man ever having been in love before. On the trail she had grown attached to him. Never had she met a man so quietly considerate, so kind to the horses — in a land where men were notoriously brutal — and so ready to smile and enjoy a joke. So brave, too, because even now he must still have been suffering from the effects of that short but savage encounter with those hard-drinking miners.

Then, as he came proudly up with his bargains, she wondered what it was that impelled him to risk his neck in a return to Kansas State.

They took the trail at greater speed after leaving Austin, and their spirits rose as the miles fled by under their hardy, prairie-bred mounts. When night came, they camped by the trail, rolling into blankets on opposite sides of the fire that the cold night in the open demanded as a necessity. With dawn, shivering in the icy wind that swept across this sometimes blazing-hot desert, they were out — Ann cooking breakfast while her companion packed up, ready for a quick move on.

And so they came at last in sight of the great salt flats — those miles and miles of pure white salt that lay, flat as a billiards table, as far as the eye could reach. There was a well-marked trail to follow, but Jack Irons could tell her of the time, just over ten years ago, when he had come riding out with the first of the forty-niners on their way to the new Californian gold-diggings, and the way he'd come, from the south, there hadn't been a trail to guide him.

'We rode by the sun,' he told her. 'We didn't know how far across it was, this salt flat, an' we just kept prayin' our water wouldn't run out.'

He got off and dug a hole. There was

an inch or so of pure white salt, then about nine inches of yellow soil, and then he came to pure white salt again.

'Interestin'?' he smiled, remounting. She nodded. 'But it doesn't get us on our way,' he told her. She wanted suddenly to tell him that her mind was divided in her need for haste. She wanted to get back to her mother as quickly as possible, true, but she didn't want that moment of parting with her trail companion in Salt Lake City.

It gave her a shock sometimes when she realized how fond she was growing of Cattleman Jack Irons — and then remembered that he was wanted in a state on a charge of brutal murder. Sometimes at night she lay and thought about it and wondered and worried — and then went to sleep in the beginnings of a despair.

Salt Lake City. The most beautiful, orderly city in all America, though still only ten years old. Every street at right angles to each other, with straight roads four miles long and over thirty yards wide — with twenty-foot sidewalks and an irrigation stream of clean, sweet water alongside every walk, bringing luxuriant life to the flowering shrubs that made the city one vast garden. The girl had never seen anything like it before.

But Iron Jack wasn't in the mood for loitering. He rode straight to a stable close by the Bowery, that big place of worship that could accommodate three thousand people, and he sold Ann's horse without much heart for bargaining. Then, leading his own travel-stained mount by the bridle, he walked with the girl to the stage-line office.

There were many glances from the Mormon population as they walked down the street together, though most were directed at the bonny, fair-haired girl who wore man's clothing. Ann told him, in answer to his question, that she didn't mind; she wouldn't buy any women's clothes. For the long journey ahead these pants were more suitable.

Then they said goodbye. Iron Jack

tried to make it brief. When he'd got her ticket written out he pushed it into her hand, along with the spare money he'd been carrying for her.

'We say goodbye here, Ann,' he growled. 'I hate to do it, so I'll say it quick. Goodbye — an' God bless you.' He swung up on to his horse and immediately galloped it away, heading out for the old Mormon Trail that led into Nebraska by way of Fort Bridger and Sterling. As he spurred out of town he thought that she stood there looking after him, and he thought that the girl was crying and he didn't like to think that he might be the cause of her tears. But he didn't turn back. He knew he couldn't. His own heart was breaking at the parting.

So he spurred on, surprising his horse by his demands for speed, and he tried to think of the Pony Express which might shortly be flying on wings of speed over this very same trail. And for once it ceased to seem romantic — it had no thrill or savour, and right then it wouldn't have mattered to him if he'd been told that the dream would never be realized.

He would have given all his hopes and ambitions with regard to the Pony Express if he could have but one more hour with the girl along the trail. Drooping in his saddle, he thought that never in his life had he spent so many happy hours as he had done with the girl, in spite of the cold and the wind and the hardness of the trail. Now, journeying alone across the vast continent of America seemed intolerable.

Intolerable or not, he had to make the journey. Ann couldn't go riding with him all her life — not with a man wanted for murder in another state. And he had to go on because there was the Pony Express — and someone he had to see in Kansas City.

* * *

By nightfall he was high up in the Wasatch Range, the first of the mighty

Rocky Mountains that he had to cross. This part of his journey would be the hardest especially at this time of the year; for he could see the white-covered mountains ahead looming like a great white barrier into the grey, snow-filled December sky. Crossing would be hardship, with peril all the way, and he felt suddenly glad that Ann would be travelling in the comparative comfort of a stage-coach.

That night he failed to find a habitation on the trail, though prudence suggested that at this height it was undesirable to sleep out. The wind had dropped, however, and so he built a big fire in a coulee, and then laced a brush screen in the manner of the Siwashers across the Canadian Border. He felt that he would be all right for the night, unless snow, accompanied by wind, came up.

He ate, but didn't enjoy his food. Then he sat staring into the fire. And he was lonely — for the first night for around a week he was without the company of Ann, and he missed her.

When he heard horse's hooves ringing along the trail he could hardly be bothered to raise his head, he was so sick with misery. When he did, it was to see a solitary horse and rider wearily walking into the firelight glow.

He came to his feet.

The rider dismounted and came walking forward. Short for a man, shapeless in too-big clothing. Then a flame spurted and he saw the face under the battered old hat that he had bought back in Austin.

Ann came forward, tremulously, her eyes watching him as if in agony — as if expecting reproof or possibly even anger from this man whom she had never known to get angry.

Irons' heart was leaping, hurting; his breath came sharply, as if he had been exerting himself suddenly. But there was joy inside him. He knew without being told what had happened.

She had been crying, watching him ride out from the Mormon city, and she must have felt as lonely as he had. Before the stage had come to take her through to Denver, she had found it intolerable — had got her money back on her ticket and bought a horse and followed him.

He looked at the horse. It was the same horse that she had ridden from Austin. Frisky young Nibbler, called thus because he took a nibble at everything, even including any garments that were left lying about. In his joy he looked at the horse as if it was an old friend.

Ann halted on the edge of the fire. She was too full for words.

Irons walked round and took her hands. 'Reckon you'll be tired, chasin' me the way I went,' he said, making his voice as casual as possible. 'I'll rustle you some supper. You sit down an' rest, dear.'

She seemed to crumple in his arms, and then she sat cross-legged before the warm, cheerful fire and cried into her hands while her companion prepared food for her supper.

5

On the outskirts of Leavenworth, Kansas, close by where a new, wooden, two-storeyed prison block had been erected, were the yards and stables of the big, expanding firm of freight hauliers and stage coach proprietors, Russell, Majors & Waddell.

At times as many as ten thousand oxen were to be seen on the land around the stables owned by the firm — ten thousand draught oxen just waiting for work to keep them occupied.

Just now the yards and adjacent fields were crammed with beasts, and it was no pleasant sight for the senior partner in the firm as he looked out at them from his office window. It made him irritable, and because he wanted to vent his irritation on something he decided to get angry at the knot of loungers sitting on the corral fences along the road in from the West.

'Goldarn it,' he exclaimed wrathfully, 'there's some fellars bin sittin' on them rails this last four days or more. Next time I go out, I'll kick 'em clear off my land.'

But he didn't go out immediately. Instead he slumped into the massive chair behind his desk, and watched from a distance the crowded inactivity of the company's yards.

Alexander Majors spoke. He was as thin as the senior partner was heavy. A good man with his brain, Alex Majors, and the man responsible for much of the company's fantastic growth in recent years.

'What're we goin' to do about it, Will?'

Waddell, the third partner, gave his opinion. 'Let's sell — now.'

But heavy, middle-aged Will Russell didn't want to sell. He growled: 'We've built this business up to a size no one's ever seen in the Middle West before.

We've become the biggest freight hauliers anywhere between here an' Salt Lake City — aye, an' we've got some pretty profitable stage lines operatin', too.'

'But,' said Waddell brutally, 'we've also got ten thousand an' more head of oxen eatin' away the profits of the past few years. Sure we're big, Will, and I hand it to you for buildin' us up this way. But we're kinda over-reachin' ourselves right now, don't you think? We've got more organization than work since the Array contract expired.'

The Mormon war had caused the firm to expand tremendously in the past two years, but now that peace had been declared in Utah there was no more profitable freight haulage to be done for the US Army. The wagons and draught oxen that had been bought to meet the needs of war were now largely on their hands.

Waddell was insistent that they should be content with the undeniably big profits of the past few years, and scale down the size of their organization to match the work they had for it.

But Russell, and to a lesser extent Alex Majors, didn't want to reverse the processes of recent years. Russell wanted to go on expanding, growing ever bigger. He didn't want to sell off stock and wagons and so reduce themselves in size.

'Don't you see,' he growled, 'if someone buys draught oxen an' wagons, what are they goin' to do with them? Why, start haulin' freight, either their own or other people's, and either way it hits us. If we start to sell, right now we start up competitors agen us.'

He rose and paced the small, bare office, then went and stood with his back to the big wood stove in one corner.

'Whatever we do seems wrong,' he growled again, and his eyebrows seemed to twitch angrily. 'Now, if only we could find a new outlet for our capital an' organization.'

He was still speaking when a knock came to the door that led directly out on to the yard. Impatiently he bellowed: 'Come in,' but as always the door stuck when the person outside tried to open it.

Russell growled: 'Blast that door. Why doesn't someone fix it?' Then went across and lifted it slightly, and the door swung open.

A tall, lean, travel-stained man stood outside. To the three partners he looked like any other hard-riding cowpuncher, and Russell demanded, shortly: 'What're you wantin' here? A job? I've got more men than work for 'em, so you'll be wastin' your time if that's what you're after.'

The tall cattleman shook his head good-humouredly, and without invitation strode into the office. Russell slammed the door behind him. His tone brightened a little, became more courteous.

'If it's haulage — ?'

'It's haulage, in a way,' nodded Iron Jack. 'Haulin' mail two-thirds o' the way across the continent.'

Alex Majors said, pleasantly: 'Mebbe

you'd better sit down an' tell us about it, stranger. First, what's your name?'

Iron Jack's eyelids flickered, then he answered: 'Jack.'

'Jack? What else?'

'Just Jack.'

'All right, Mister Just Jack. Who d'you represent?'

'I've come from Senator William Gwin, of California.'

The three partners were listening intently now. 'Senator Gwin wants you to do something that Congress won't attempt.'

'What's that?' growled Russell.

'Senator Gwin wants to start a Pony Express from St. Joseph to Sacramento or San Francisco. He's been to Congress to try to get them to subsidize the line, but they just laugh at the idea. They say it isn't possible for mail to be carried by a fast relay of riders a distance of nigh on two thousand miles in about ten days.' Suddenly a question rapped out — 'What's your opinion, gentlemen?'

150

The gentlemen looked at each other. Then Waddell spoke. 'They don't know hosses — or Westerners,' was all he said.

Irons sighed. He had a feeling that with that confident statement he had suddenly progressed half-way towards getting this idea accepted.

Waddell asked, point blank: 'Why come to us? Why not to some other firm of freight haulers?'

'You're a Kansas firm, with head-quarters here and in Atchison. The railhead from the East terminates at St. Joseph, more than a river's width from Atchison.' Iron Jack leaned forward now, suddenly determined to talk them into the project.

'Look, you've got stations an' depots all the way across Kansas to Colorado, an' Nebraska as far as Salt Lake City. You've got the stations for the Pony Express changes — Congress would have had to establish their own if they'd backed the idea, an' that would have landed 'em into a big outlay of money.'

151

'This idea seems to demand a lot from our firm, as it is,' said Russell drily.

'You've got the men, you've got the hosses, an' you've got the chain of stations right across to Salt Lake City,' Iron Jack argued. 'Fix a few more stations into California and spread your freightin' business right on to the Pacific Coast. Right now they're hauling thousands of tons of supplies to the big silver workings around Virginia City. I reckon a firm as big as yours could get a nice slab of that work.'

He stopped. The three partners were curiously silent, watching him intently.

Iron Jack asked ironically: 'Did I say somethin'?'

Heavy old Will Russell stirred. 'You sure did, Mr Just Jack. Now, you tell us about this business developin' across the Rockies. We've had news of it, but maybe if you've been through Nevada lately you'll be able to tell us the size of it.' He exchanged quick glances with his partners.

So Iron jack told him all he knew about the haulage on the west coast; how wagon trains left the docks and quays by the hundred every week during the dry months of the year, and how mine-owners across the Nevadas would pay fantastic prices to get the supplies they needed to open up new workings.

'They're askin' a hundred dollars a ton for full loads to freight goods a hundred and fifty miles from California to Virginia City,' he told them, and saw their eyes widen at the information. 'Aye, an' at the rate of two hundred dollars a ton for small loads.' He told them that one firm he knew in Virginia City paid ten thousand dollars a month in freightage, so clearly there was big money for a firm like Russell, Majors & Waddell in the Sierras.

At length Russell rose and walked to the window and looked out upon the vast yards with their lowing herds of draught oxen. Here was a chance to use his beasts without selling them off to make possible competitors. As he was turning he suddenly realized that those loungers weren't on the corral rails any more — the first time in days that they'd moved — and he vaguely wondered at it.

But then he came back and stood over Iron Jack and said: 'You're talkin' us into it, Mister Just Jack. I c'n see if we keep talkin' with you we'll own two thousand miles of Pony Express route!'

Irons came up out of his chair at that. 'If talk's all that's needed, I'll stay talkin' until them steers out there get calves,' he vowed, and the three partners laughed.

When they were all seated round the desk again, the former Texas Ranger began to go into the details of the scheme. Senator Gwin's idea was spectacular — too spectacular for orthodox business men — but basically it was sound. Men on both coasts were willing to pay well to any carrier of speedily delivered mails, and the proposal Senator Gwin had made, of a fee of five dollars per letter, promised good revenue to the Pony Express.

There were arguments against the scheme — Waddell especially after a time became less enthusiastic — but Russell and Alex Majors plainly liked the idea. In time Jack Irons was able to sit back and let that pair work out the solutions to many of the problems.

At length Will Russell rose and said: 'Wal, Mister Just Jack, you'll have to leave us to talk it over. I don't mind tellin' you that I like the idea, but I c'n see a few hundred thousand dollars havin' to be sunk into this project before we start to earn money, and no man does that in a hurry, I guess. You come again, this time tomorow, an' we'll talk more about the matter.'

He shook hands with the cattleman, as did Majors and Waddell; then Irons moved across towards the door. Russell spoke drily: 'Mebbe now you'll tell us what fits on to the Jack part o' your name, mister.' Irons halted and turned. Russell was looking closely at him. 'I've kinda got an idea I've seen your face around before.'

Irons said, easily: 'Sure you have. I've passed you more times than I c'n count. That's why I thought of you when Senator Gwin wanted someone to back his scheme.'

He lifted the latch and tried to open the plank door, but it wouldn't move. Russell stepped forward hastily.

'The blamed thing sticks,' he said wrathfully. 'I'll get it fixed today — soon as you've gone, mister. The damn' door!'

He wrestled a moment and then the door flew open.

A gun jabbed forward into Russell's stomach. Round the door-edge Irons saw a group of men crouched outside the doorway. The one with the gun wore a star on his chest. Back of him were two scrub-faced men who looked remotely familiar.

And with them was the smiling, insolent Rolly Weyte — Rowlands, as he had been known, back here in Kansas six years before.

The sheriff's eyes came wider, startled at sight of the familiar Russell at the end of his gun. Then he tried to push past the freight hauler, but Russell had bulk and that wasn't easy. Also, quite naturally, Russell was beginning to show signs of indignation.

'What the — ' he roared. The sheriff came lurching through the doorway. Then stopped. He saw a long-barrelled Colt threatening him — saw a lean, tough-looking *hombre* crouched back of it.

Weyte saw him, too, and shouted: 'That's him! That's Iron Jack, *the woman-killer*!'

His gun was flaming even before he had finished speaking. Then Jack Irons' Colt roared, making the dust dance on the board floor and the lamp to swing behind the desk.

Both were snap shots; both at targets moving evasively. Neither bullet hit. Then Irons jumped feet first through the window, taking the frame and glass out with him with a tremendous shattering sound.

Russell and his partners were shouting, surprised and indignant. The sheriff and the other three men rushed into the office, ignoring the owners, and opened up after Irons. He was climbing the rail around an ox corral, and before they could hit him he had dropped in among the plunging, frightened beasts and was lost to sight.

Rowlands took the lead. 'Outside,' he shouted. 'Get mounted and circle them corrals. An' shoot to kill! Iron Jack's a killer, I tell you!'

Jack Irons knew he was in a tight corner when he dropped into that corral. This was running away from his horse, but his mount unfortunately was hitched to the rail right outside the door by which Rowlands and the sheriff had come. With those bullets chasing him, he just had to go whichever way he could.

The draught oxen in the corral for the moment gave him cover. He ran as fast as he could, threading his way through the startled, snorting, saliva-drooling beasts, and slipped through the rails of an adjoining corral. His sudden appearance scared the normally placid oxen, and they started to mill around in panic, their long horns tossing, their big brown eyes wild and showing rolling whites. It became dangerous, within the confined space of the corral, to be in among those big brutes, and Irons was near to being knocked down and trampled on several times.

And when he came out by the far rail, it was in time to see Rowlands and his two henchmen in the act of riding up alongside the corral fence.

He was trapped. They had him penned inside with the oxen, and if they spread out and kept circling the corral, they could keep him prisoner until he gave up in despair or went under those sharp, trampling hoofs when exhaustion claimed him.

Over the lurching red-brown backs Irons saw Rowlands riding right up against the fence. Rowlands didn't spot him. He saw the Californian goldmine-owner raise his gun and deliberately fire in among the beasts. Rowlands shouted something, and at that the two scrub-faced men came into view and they too started to fire their revolvers in among the cattle.

Irons wanted to shout out in alarm, foreseeing the result. Those deafening, blazing guns would panic the beasts and they would rush around in blind fear, injuring and even killing each other in their efforts to get away from the cause of their panic. And he realized that he wouldn't stand a chance once the panic started — within a little time these great, plunging bodies would have him off his feet, and he would be trampled to death in no time.

That, of course, was Rowlands' plan. Rowlands wanted him out of the way — wanted to kill him, and the quicker the better. And getting him trampled to death inside this corral was as good a way as any.

These and other thoughts flashed

through the cattleman's mind the moment the firing started. The next moment it seemed that all hell erupted around him.

Maddened beasts bellowed in the high, quick-snorting way that panic-stricken oxen do. They reared on their hind legs, looming a good eight feet above the cattleman, their forefeet stabbing wildly as if at their unseen fears.

Then the rush away to the far fence started, Irons going with the beasts, frantically dodging their unwieldy bodies and slashing hoofs. Once he was bowled into the dust before a charge of young, nimble oxen, but in some miraculous way he rolled on to his feet and swayed beyond range of a row of tossing horns.

The oxen hit the far fence, piled up in a savage, roaring press of beef, and then seemed to rebound and come charging back across the corral again. Irons knew this would go on — this mad charging from side to side of the corral — until the oxen were too exhausted to run another stride. By that time most of them would be severely hurt, and many would be dead. Irons had seen stampedes in corrals before and knew what they were like.

Even now, as the tide flowed away from the north fence, there were a lot of oxen down on their sides, legs kicking, flanks slashed open and pouring with blood. This stampede that Rowlands had deliberately started was going to cost the firm of Russell, Majors & Waddell quite an amount.

He tried to keep out from the throng of maddened cattle, tried to hang on their heels out in the open, but one of the riders outside the fence must have come racing round, and immediately he opened fire on the cattleman. Whether he liked it or not, Irons had to plunge in again among the milling, bellowing beasts, if only to live a few seconds longer.

Then the charge of crazy oxen hit the south fence, and seemed to be reflected back against it. All in one moment Irons found himself at the head of five hundred beasts all intent on impaling themselves against the north fence again. Irons ran like lightning, trying to keep ahead of the oxen and yet not get too far ahead so that he showed as a target to be shot at. Then, twenty yards from the fence he sprinted, jumping the moaning beasts that had gone down under the first charge, and climbing on to the wide gate.

He got the bar out as the first of the bellowing cattle crashed into the rails, pressed on by the fear-maddened beasts behind. The second bar started to come — and then stuck. Rowlands was riding up hell for leather to get within pistol range of him. A fortunate milling of beasts kept the gate clear for a second. In that second Irons heaved, and the bar came out. Clinging to it, Irons felt the big gate quiver and then begin to swing open.

And then the flood of oxen hit the fence, and some found the opening as the gate swung outwards. In a moment the river of oxen was pouring out on to the trail that led into Leavenworth; men were racing up from all directions, a few of them mounted, but they might just as well have tried to stop a prairie fire with their bare hands, for all the good they could do right then.

Irons clung to the gate; the breath knocked out of his body as the clumsy animals crashed by against him. Then he saw his chance and jumped — landed on a broad back and lay clinging there.

He was a mile on his way into Leavenworth before he could leap off the ox's back and run for cover into the undergrowth by the side of the trail. He lay there on the hillside, watching the tiring beasts flounder on, still helplessly gripped by their panic.

Back in the far distance he saw riders in among the stricken cattle inside the corral, and he thought: 'That'll be Rowlands — him and his friends. They'll be lookin' for my corpse among them dyin' cattle.'

Well, they wouldn't find him there. He had been lucky; he had managed to escape alive from that raging pit of madness. But it had been luck — luck and quick thinking when he'd spotted that gate. Rowlands was going to be disappointed, and that would make him vicious.

His breath coming more easily now, Jack Irons sat up and gave further thought to his position.

That sheriff who had been lurking outside the office door must have been brought in by Rowlands to arrest him. It meant that the law in Kansas State knew about his presence here, so that he could expect to be hunted viciously whilst he remained in the territory. He had hoped to complete his business, here in Kansas, without being recognized, but Rowlands had upset his plan. Now it meant that if he stayed to carry out the plans that had brought him here, he did so only at the risk of his life.

The thought of crossing the border into some state where Kansas law didn't operate never occurred to him. He had come to Kansas on two missions — he would complete both of them before going away again.

Cautiously he made his way towards the town, keeping well back from the winding, dust-laden trail down which the red-brown oxen were still careering. Again he looked back at the corrals. A posse of horsemen was galloping after the escaping cattle; no doubt they would be Russell's men, intent on rounding up the stampeders, but he thought Rowlands and his two scrub-faced friends might be among them so he plunged deeper into the bush.

Thought of those scrub-faced companions of his enemy sent his face into a puckering frown. He had a feeling that he had met with those men before — he felt that he should remember who they were, that in some way it was important that he should recall the circumstances of some other meeting with them. But for the moment he couldn't remember.

After a time he stopped trying to remember, and instead gave his thoughts to the need for escape. That meant that in some way he had to get a horse. He had little enough money left — not enough to buy a horse, anyway — and, in any event he was sure that any time now the Law would be watching sellers of horses, knowing him to have escaped without his own mount.

He sighed. He didn't want to do it, but it seemed the best thing for him would be to steal a horse from the Russell outfit . . .

He saw a cowboy threading his way through the bush in search of strays. When that cowboy came out into a clearing it was to see a tall, lean, hard-lookin' *hombre* standing wide-legged before him. The said hard-lookin' *hombre* carried a hard-lookin' Colt in his right hand.

Irons said: 'Sorry, pardner. I need that hoss more'n you do.'

The cowboy looked reflectively at that Colt, his hands climbing slowly above his sweat-stained hat. 'You Iron Jack?' he asked politely. The cattleman nodded. 'Then,' said the cowboy with resignation, 'I reckon you do.'

He started to swing down out of his saddle. Then he seemed to fall away from it, and Irons caught the flash of gun metal as a swiftly drawn six-shooter arced in the waning afternoon light.

Irons risked hitting the horse. He pulled trigger — once. The heavy bullet kicked flesh out of the cowboy's forearm, and he yelped and dropped his gun before it could be levelled at the cattleman. Irons walked slowly over and picked up the Colt.

'I didn't want to have to do that, fellar,' he said. 'But you'd have plugged me, wouldn't you?'

The cowboy was a philosopher. 'Yeah, I reckon I would. I took a chance.' He shrugged. 'It didn't come off.' Then he added: 'I reckon there's many a gun goin' to come up shootin' at you while there's a five-hundred-dollar bounty placed on your head.'

'Five hundred dollars?' Irons was startled. Then he said, with grim humour: 'The last I heard, my scalp was only worth two hundred dollars. Now it's five hundred!'

'Sure.' The cowboy rolled back his sleeve and inspected the wound. 'There's a fellar called Weyte back up at Russell's says he'll add three hundred dollars to the pile if you get caught — or brought in dead. He don't care which way.'

'Weyte?' Irons fixed a piece of cloth around the wound for the injured cowboy. 'He sure is determined to get me out of the way,' he thought. But if he, Irons, died, maybe all chance of Rowlands having to suffer for the Belle Storr crime might die with him, he remembered. A man's life was well worth three hundred dollars, especially if you had as much money as the goldmine-owner.

Irons swung into the saddle. The cowboy watched him mount regretfully. 'Tell your boss I'm only borrowin' this hoss,' he told the man. 'Tell him I'll return it or pay for it at one of the Russell stations out West.'

The cowboy said: 'Sure I'll tell him,' but plainly he didn't believe what Irons was saying.

Then the cattleman swung away and went riding in a circle round the town. He went and hid in a wood that came thickly down to the edge of the Missouri. There he slept, hungry. Next morning he got some food off some boatmen poling north, and then, early in the afternoon, quite openly rode back round Leavenworth and cantered up to the Russell office that he had visited the previous day.

The corral had been tidied up, but there was plenty of evidence of the stampede all along the trail. The office, too, was operating with a board across where a window had been the previous day.

But Will Russell evidently had had the door fixed, for when Irons pressed the latch it swung open easily.

He stood silently in the doorway, looking in. The three partners sat just as silently around Will Russell's desk and looked back at him. Then Will Russell got impatient and said: 'All right, come in. There's no trap set for you, fellar.' He looked at his partners triumphantly. 'They said you wouldn't come back, but I bet you would.'

Irons shut the door and went across to the chair he had occupied the previous day. He felt that he was, if not among friends, at least not in the midst of vicious, hating enemies. All the same, he sat with his hand near to his gun butt, and his eyes were careful to note every movement of the men before him.

He drawled: 'Reckon I sure owe you an apology for stealin' one of your men's hosses — it was your hoss, I reckon.'

'Our hoss,' agreed Russell, nodding, his eyes just as intent on the cattleman. 'You don't need to worry about that, though.' He glanced at his partners quickly. 'Mebbe we owe you something,' he said.

Irons seemed to stiffen in his chair, as if a barely suppressed excitement

171

gripped him. 'You mean — '

'We're aimin' to go further with Senator Gwin's idea of a Pony Express. We're already sendin' riders down along the line, arrangin' rest and way stations. Alex here is goin' off on a buyin' trip — buyin' the finest hosses in America.' Alex Majors rose at that and said: 'We've sure worked fast while you've been away, Iron Jack. You wait here a minute; you'll see the first of the Pony Express riders go into action.'

But Jack Irons' Colt said: 'No.' Majors halted, surprised, as blue steel flashed into the cattleman's brown, sinewy hand. Irons said, softly: 'Mebbe you'd better sit down agen, Mr Majors. You reminded me I'm Iron Jack in Kansas. I can't run any risks that you might go out an' get a sheriff like Rowlands did yesterday. Nope. I'm gonna be the first man to leave this office, I guess.'

Big, heavy Will Russell was watching Iron Jack under bushed-up brows. He spoke slowly. 'You c'n put that gun away, Iron Jack. Alex didn't mean any harm to you. Let him go an' you'll see somethin' you've been wantin' to see for a long time.' But Irons never moved; the Colt sat just as squarely in that steady hand. So Russell tried again.

'You never killed that gal, did you, Jack?' Iron Jack didn't answer. 'There's a lot of people here in Kansas swore you couldn't have done it. You were brought up with Belle, weren't you? Like brother an' sister. You don't look the kind of man to do a wild thing like killin' someone as close to you as that.'

Iron Jack's voice grated: 'I didn't kill her — you're right on that point. I don't know who killed her for sure, but in the last years I've begun to suspect Rowlands. Now I can't see that it could be anyone else. But suspectin' Rowlands doesn't help me. With that five-hundred-dollar reward offered I'll be shot on sight by any of thousands of reward hunters. Dead or alive, Rowlands said, didn't he?'

Russell nodded.

Iron Jack said, harshly: 'That's a great encouragement to make sure I'm brought in dead. That, I figure, is Rowlands' idea. He doesn't want me around, openin' my mouth to accuse him. The sooner I'm dead an' out of the way, the sooner he c'n stop worryin' about justice catchin' up with him over Beale Storr's murder.'

Russell seemed to nod slightly, as if in agreement. 'Mebbe you're right, Jack. One thing you c'n bet on, though, an' that is — we don't believe this charge agen you. We've met you, an' we can't see how it's possible for you to have killed a gal.'

Iron Jack seemed to sigh, then his gun went slowly back into its holster. Alex Majors went out.

Russell went on talking. 'We don't know that last, vital leg of the journey from Salt Lake City to the Pacific Coast. You seem to know it well.'

'Like a book,' Iron Jack nodded.

'OK, then, will you take over that section of the Pony Express route for us? Go out there an' fix rest an' way stations all the way from Salt Lake City. Buy your own hosses, engage your own riders an' station hands — make every arrangement for collectin' an' deliverin' Government mail. We'll give you a letter to our Salt Lake City manager, who'll supply you with funds as you require them.'

Iron Jack's heart leapt, but his face seemed as impassive as ever. 'I'll take on the job,' he drawled. 'Kansas law doesn't operate so far West, so I'll be able to work openly for you. Give me three months an' you c'n start off your Pony Express — '

Waddell grinned: 'It's already started. Look, here he comes. Yippee!'

They crowded to the doorway at the sound of rapidly approaching hoofs. Iron Jack saw a horseman rocketing along the trail from the Russell stables. One moment it was a small, black, swaying dot; the next it resolved itself into a mighty gleaming black stallion that hurled itself towards them. A second later and it was past and a shower of gravel from its flying hooves spattered the wooden-walled office building, the dust rose, biting into their nostrils, and they scarcely saw that small, clinging form on the back of the mighty charger.

Iron Jack saw a rather small, lean cowboy: hat brim flattened across his head before the pressure of wind, lightly clad in shirt and trousers tucked into small, cutaway boots, sitting a saddle unlike any saddle he had ever seen before.

Russell demanded, triumphantly: 'What d'you think of that, Jack?'

Iron Jack said: 'I'd give every penny I have to own that hoss. With hosses like that, the Pony Express can't fail.'

Waddell looked at his partner, then smiled: 'We want you to get back to the Pacific Coast in good time, Jack, so — take that hoss from the firm of Russell, Majors & Waddell to help you make record time!'

Alex Majors came riding back along

the trail at that moment, cutting short Irons' astonished thanks, and then the cowboy came back with the mighty black horse, and they all stood around and examined it.

Waddell took off the saddle for Irons to see. It was a racing saddle that they'd had in the stables for years, one brought in by some immigrant from England. To the cattleman, used especially to the high-pommelled Mexican and Texas saddles, it looked curiously inadequate, a mere wafer of leather, and yet he recognized it as completely adequate and a great saving in weight. The blanket, too, was so small that it scarcely showed under the saddle.

'We'll have to make equipment as light as possible,' Waddell said. 'Every ounce becomes vital when hosses have to carry it nearly two thousand miles. We'll send you your supplies to our manager in Salt Lake City in time for the route to be opened, Jack.'

Then they put a more orthodox saddle on to the black horse, and Irons mounted. 'You goin' West right away, Jack?' Russell queried. But Irons shook his head.

'There's one important job I've still to do,' he told them, but he didn't say it meant a visit to Kansas City, where many people would know him.

'Good luck,' they called. And Alex Majors shouted: 'Keep your hand near your gun, Jack — an' take care!'

He rode away, and the sweet rhythm of those mighty striding legs was an experience new in the life of the cattleman, though he'd ridden some of the best horses along the Border. This was a horse among horses.

'It's just . . . black lightning,' he marvelled, as they followed the river road towards Kansas, and from that moment that was his horse's name — Black Lightning.

Two hours later Iron Jack ran into a pair of scrub-faced men — and remembered where he had first met up with them.

6

He was approaching the fork of the Kansas and Missouri rivers when he encountered the pair. And his thoughts were on the girl who had been his good companion over eighteen hundred miles of trail. Ann Caudry was rarely out of his thoughts these days.

They had parted at Topeka, Ann to ride east the few miles to her home on the outskirts of Kansas City, Irons to strike north to the town of Leavenworth, head-quarters of the Russell firm.

It had been a sorrowful parting. Now that she was so near to home Ann's anxiety for her mother had increased, so that she had little thought for anything except the urgent need to race to her side, if she still lived. On the last stages of their journey she had spoken little, and then usually about her mother.

At the ford on the Kansas River they had parted. Iron Jack said simply: 'I hope things are all right, Ann. Anyway, you couldn't have got to your mother's side any faster.'

'Thanks to you,' smiled the girl. She turned in her saddle, and it seemed that her glance was wistful as she looked back along the trail that had been so hard and yet had given her many happy hours with this strong, trustworthy cattleman.

'It's all over now,' Irons smiled.

'Yes, all over, Jack. Perhaps someday we'll take the trail again together.' There was a lump in her throat. She knew it was unlikely. If her mother was ill she would have to remain with her in Kansas, and Iron Jack was a wanted man in that State and wouldn't be able to stay with her. No, this was the parting, and they both knew it.

They smiled and shook hands, and then Irons put his horse into the water and splashed his way across to the north bank. When he looked back Ann was riding slowly along the river bank, very small on her large-boned horse, a quaint figure in her too-big man's clothing. She looked incredibly forlorn, and Jack Irons had to tear his eyes away because it hurt to see her in her loneliness.

And he knew his heart was breaking as he widened the distance between himself and the girl he loved. For he had grown to love her on that long trail, and he felt that any man must have fallen in love with a girl like Ann Caudry, if he were by her side for the better part of a month, as he himself had been.

There was a tavern along the road into Kansas City, just on the edge of the river. It was a poor place, set back among some stumps where trees had been felled away from the trail. Irons decided to eat in this isolated place rather than try for food in the city itself, and he turned across towards the primitive house.

The floor was hard-packed earth, and

inside smelt damp and cold from the earth walls, but Irons remembered this place and knew that a good, if not fancy, meal could be obtained here. He didn't think the proprietor would recognize him after all this time, so he walked in confidently.

Then he stopped. A bill was tacked to a supporting post just within the doorway. He looked at it. It said

$500 REWARD
will be paid for the
body, dead or alive, of
IRON JACK
notorious woman slayer

Then followed an accurate description of Jack Irons, along with the information that he was known to have returned to Kansas and 'might try to re-visit his old haunts.'

That latter statement made Iron Jack bite his lip in annoyance. For that was precisely his intention, and now it meant that if he tried to complete his mission it would be only at the greatest risk of his life.

Frowning, he turned away. Two scrub-faced men stepped away from the darkness of the unwindowed walling. They had guns in their hands, and somehow they looked particularly menacing. Iron Jack had a feeling that those trigger fingers were itching.

One of the men growled furtively to the other: 'It's him. Let's blow him apart — it's safer!'

Hearing that voice, Iron Jack suddenly remembered something — the snowy trail leading into the Sierra Nevada Mountains, two men riding slowly ahead of him . . . two men who had planned to hold him up and rob him.

Or had they?

His thoughts raced. These men had been with Rowlands and the sheriff yesterday; they must have come with his enemy across the continent. If that were so, then these were no ordinary stick-up men. He began to think: 'There's more to it than meets the eye. These men weren't on that trail that day to rob me!'

Then, if his hunch was right, if they hadn't intended to rob him, they could have intended only one thing — to kill him by the trail side!

A voice shouted: 'Put them guns away, blast you!' Just as Irons was thinking: 'Why should they want to kill me? They don't know me — I've never done anything to them before.' And somehow the instant theory that they were paid murderers of Rowlands didn't quite fit the bill . . .

The tavern proprietor, a big, red-faced, ruffianly-looking man himself, had a shotgun out and pointing at them. He was used to tough men, especially men who came in from the river, who thought that a fight should accompany every bottle of rye whiskey. Sight of those flashing guns was enough for him.

'I do the shootin' around here,' he trumpeted. 'Nobody kills nobody 'cept me, see?'

The Colts went down, sullenly, reluctantly. Irons took a step back towards the door. One of the scrub-faced men got desperate. 'The hell, don't you see who this is? It's Iron Jack, the murderer. Let's split that five-hundred-dollar reward — '

Iron Jack jumped sideways. Two Colts leapt up at the beginning of the movement and flamed bullets through the doorway. The proprietor saw five hundred good dollars on the run away from him and came scrambling over the rude counter with his shotgun.

But Iron Jack was away, leaping into his saddle, bending and expertly pulling the reins loose with one tug, then racing across among the tree stumps out of pistol range. The shotgun roared; a few pieces of lead zipped by him, but if any hit the horse they must have been spent and didn't seem to be noticed by the magnificent black.

Irons crouched low in the saddle and nursed his long-striding horse around the tricky bends of the river road.

Behind him, but growing fainter, was the sound of pursuing hoofs.

He was now on the outskirts of Kansas City — that part of Kansas City, anyway, that lay on the west bank of the broad Missouri. He thought: 'If I go into the city I'll be trapped.' Once it was known he was inside the town they would cordon it off, and then make a systematic search for him, from house to house.

He made a brief gesture of impatience, riding swiftly down that trail. He had come all this way from California on a mission, to see someone here in Kansas City, and now, because he had been followed from Sacramento by his enemy, Rowlands, it seemed that he would be prevented from attaining his end. It was bitterly disappointing, but there was no use fretting, he knew, and instantly he altered his plans.

He tried to shake the pursuers off by leaping a fence and riding across country over a rolling brow of a hill. He almost succeeded. He was just going over the skyline when they came rocketing along the river trail. He heard shouts, turned and saw them clumsily leaping the fence that his own magnificent black had cleared with ease, and groaned. Then he settled down to some hard riding among the scattered copses of trees that fringed the west sector of the town. If he could throw off the pursuit — perhaps at the same time letting them believe that his mission lay beyond Kansas City and not within it — he might later find a chance of sneaking into the town and completing his mission.

Suddenly he reined. There was a house below, set among some cottonwoods against an old mill on a stream. Irons thought: 'That must be Ann's house!' She had described it to him, so that if ever he came that way he would recognize it. He had known it to be on the western outskirts of the town, but all the same he had stumbled upon it accidentally.

Instantly a tremendous yearning

came over him to see the girl once more, and he was unable to resist it. Glancing behind, it seemed that he had thrown off pursuit for the moment, so he risked sending his horse sliding down a steep bank on to a trail that led down to the porticoed, wood-and-stone residence of the Caudrys.

Galloping up to the house, he bent under the bare branches of some low-spreading fruit trees and continued round to the back quarters. There was no time for ceremony. Though he had evaded pursuit temporarily, there was no saying when his enemies might stumble upon him at this house.

He strode through a kitchen. Two women were baking bread, their arms white with flour up to their elbows. They gawked, but acting on an instinct Irons strode past them and into a passage that clearly led to the family's rooms.

He saw an open door of a pleasantly furnished sitting-room, a big log fire dancing in a wide hearth across from him.

And Ann, very erect and white, was sitting on a straight-backed chair looking unseeingly into the flames.

Irons took of his hat and walked across to her. His feet made no sound on that carpet, so that she was unaware of his approach until he was right beside her.

He saw her pale, thin face lift, her blue, misery-drenched eyes rise to meet his. She saw him, and it seemed that a gladness came to her face, that a spot of colour rose to touch her cheekbones. But she was incredulous, as if not believing her eyes. Her mouth opened to say something, but no sound emerged.

Irons was stricken, seeing her unutterable sorrow. He went down on one knee and placed his rough brown hand over both hers. In that moment he no longer looked the tough, hard cattleman that most men saw in Jack Irons.

'Your mother?' he asked softly.

'I got here in time.' She had wept a lot, he could see, and when she spoke more tears weren't far away. 'But

. . . mother's dying fast.'

Then, perhaps because now she realized how lonely she had been without him, she broke down and wept. Awkwardly he rose to his feet. The girl clung to his arm, pressing her face against his rough sleeve.

When he looked round he saw two floury-armed servant women watching, gape-mouthed and astounded, from the doorway. When his eyes fell on them, they stared a little longer, then crept back to their bread-making.

In time the girl recovered her composure a little, and then she dried her eyes and talked to him. She talked freely, hiding nothing from him — as if her trust in him was complete.

She talked of the horror of her home-coming, to find her mother lingering on the edge of death, as if determined to keep alive until her beloved daughter returned. And almost immediately after recognizing her, the frail, dying woman had fallen into a coma.

'The doctor says she might last for

weeks, or — oh, Jack, I am going to lose my mother!'

He wanted to say: 'Come to me when it is all over. I'll look after you as well as ever your mother did.' He wanted to take her into his arms and comfort her, but he knew this wasn't the time for any talk of love. If it had to come at all, that must be later . . .

They both turned as an agitated female came hurrying through the doorway. She was one of the bread-bakers. Without any ceremony she exclaimed: 'For land's sake, Miss Ann, this place sure is full of men today.'

Irons strode across. 'What do you mean? What men?'

The woman answered: 'There's a lot on hosses back among the elms, an' there's another posse strung across the trail over by the mill. Sarah says she thinks there's more in the brake down by the river.'

Ann cried: 'Oh, Jack, they're after you!'

For a second Irons stood stock still,

trying to understand how he had come to be trapped. Then light dawned. He had come upon Ann's house accidentally, but his pursuers must have assumed that his mission in Kansas City lay with this girl who had ridden across the continent with him. They must have raced off for help, and now he was ringed round with enemies who would shoot him down for the reward that his body would bring them.

'Dead or alive,' that was the offer that Rowlands had made; and Irons guessed that no one would bother much to try to get him alive.

Ann rushed out to the back, Irons close behind her. A quick survey seemed to show mounted men in all directions. Ann said: 'Give me your hat, Jack,' and she took it before he knew what she was up to. Then she raced across towards the stables, came out in a second riding a young black horse bare-backed, in a side-saddle position because of her skirt. He saw his hat hiding her curls and understood.

'Ann!' he shouted in horror, but he was too late. The girl flashed by him, racing down the trail towards the south and the river bend. Instantly the brush became alive with horsemen urging their mounts into pursuit; there was a crashing of heavy bodies in every direction, and then the hunt centred and concentrated hard on the heels of that flying black horse and rider.

The way was clear now for Irons to race off through the elms to the north, but he found himself unable to do it. He could only stand and watch after the posse that pursued the girl. He heard guns firing, and his heart leapt madly in fear for the quick-witted girl who had saved his life.

Then he saw her sweep off his hat, revealing her fair woman's curls below, and the gesture was derisive, as if saying to the baffled hunters: 'See, you've been tricked, and by a woman at that!'

He knew that no harm would come to her now they knew her identity, and instantly he sprang into the saddle of his own magnificent horse and went thundering along a pathway that led into the cover of those giant elms. Almost as soon as he felt the powerful, surging muscles of his horse beneath him he knew that he could disdain pursuit. Black Lightning would outstrip almost anything on four legs.

On a hill to the west of Kansas City, he looked down upon the thriving, Middle-West town where it sat at the junction of two brown, swirling rivers, and he thought 'I'll come back some day.'

There was his mission still to be completed — and there was Ann to bring him always to her side. But just now it was too dangerous to stay in the vicinity, and anyway he had no time to lose if he were to establish the Pacific link to the Pony Express.

He turned his horse's nose west-wards. Now to concentrate on that magic-provoking enterprise, the world's greatest relay race . . . the Pony Express!

7

There came a day when a letter awaited Jack Irons' arrival at the Russell, Majors & Waddell Offices in Salt Lake City. It said, briefly: 'The Pony Express service is scheduled to begin operation on April 3rd, 1860. On that day the first rider must leave Sacramento on his journey eastwards, just as the first rider leaves St. Joseph, Missouri, with the mail brought by train from New York. See that all arrangements are completed for that date.'

Irons dropped the letter and looked at the dry, spare, clerkly western manager and exulted: 'Yippee, we're nearly there!'

It was a wonderful moment, to realize that within three weeks the Pony Express would actually begin its dramatic history. Three weeks would see the culmination of nearly three months of hard work.

It had been a battle to cross the Rockies with his letter of introduction and instruction to the firm's Salt Lake manager, and then had come a grim business of selecting sites for way stations, where the mail riders would change mounts, and rest stations where men could sleep after their spell in the saddle.

These rest stations were fixed at intervals of about seventy miles, though a few on the easy sections ran to over a hundred miles. Way stations varied from seven miles to over ten, depending on the roughness of the terrain to be crossed.

The Pony Express riders would each ride seventy to a hundred miles at a stretch before handing over at a rest station to another man, then next day would ride back along the same route carrying mail in a reverse direction.

It would be a hard life, demanding around six hours at a stretch in the saddle for the riders — and that riding at breakneck speed the whole of the way — and employing around ten horses on each sector.

All the same, there was any number of volunteers for the coveted honour of being Pony Express riders. Men who loved horses especially wanted the jobs; for these horses that the firm had bought for the relay were the finest that money could buy. It would be a thrill to sit astride them and tear off each day along this route east and west across the continent.

Irons picked his men with great care. He wanted lightweights, men who would be no more than jockeys on the backs of their superb mounts. They would have to ride wearing the lightest of clothing, and must turn out day or night, cold, wet or fine, when it was their turn to take up the trail. Neither would they be able to carry arms.

'Every ounce is important,' he told his riders frankly. 'We get five dollars for every half-ounce letter we carry. If our riders carry guns, belts, holsters an' ammunition, how much less mail c'n we take on? Ten or even fifteen pounds weight. That means we lose over a thousand dollars in mail . . . '

They saw his point. And when they saw the superb horses that were to carry them they forgot to argue any more. Their safety would rest in the flying feet of these carefully chosen racehorses, they could see.

The weeks passed. Senator Gwin gave all the assistance that he could at the Californian end of the route, but without telegraph over the Sierras it meant a continual back-and-forward ride along the trail for Jack Irons — one day he was inspecting a rudely constructed way station with stable that had been built outside Carson City; the next he was bidding for some mighty roan or chestnut at a sale in Virginia City. And the day after that he would spend interviewing eager men who had travelled right across the state to beg for the privilege of riding for the Pony Express.

If he'd had time he would have sent

down to Texas for some of his hard-riding friends there, but there wasn't time and so he recruited all along the trail as he rode.

Then, three days before the first riders were due to make the initial run, with the interest and enthusiasm of all America upon them, a letter was brought by special messenger from Senator Gwin.

'Rolly Weyte is back on the coast,' the senator wrote. 'He's got a lot of men out at his mine — new recruits — and they're the toughest bunch of plug-uglies I've ever seen. They're not mining, and I figure he intends to use them for some other purpose. Watch out. You've got a bad enemy in Weyte, and I think he's going to turn these men against you.'

Irons put down the letter in bewilderment. Rowlands did hate him, did want him out of the way. But surely he didn't need to recruit a big gang of men to do it? An ambush with his scrub-faced pair of hoodlums would more likely be effective than an attack on the part of a gang.

Irons sat late into the night in the rest station at Carson City, trying to think of the real purpose behind the recruitment of a gang for Rowlands.

Then it began to dawn on him what it might be.

This gang wasn't so much intended for assault upon himself as upon the Pony Express system!

It took him a long time to accept this theory, because it didn't seem to fit in any direction at first. Rowlands surely had no grudge against the Express — it couldn't matter to him if it did operate . . . in fact he would benefit by a fast mail system to the east along with all other citizens in California.

And Rowlands, with all the wealth from his three mines, couldn't be contemplating stealing the government mail for what it might contain.

It was baffling. He went to sleep without understanding what was behind the manoeuvre, and yet he was completely convinced that his guess was right — Rowlands, for some reason, was aiming to stop the Pony Express from working.

Next day another fast rider came in with a message. Again it was from Senator Gwin. '*Watch out, Jack*,' it said: '*I saw Rolly Weyte ride out with his gang this morning.*'

Watch out? But for what? All Irons could do was go about the business of seeing that these vital stations in the mighty Sierra Nevada Mountains were ready when the relay race began a couple of days later.

Purposely Irons had positioned himself on the eastern slopes of the Nevadas, reckoning that if any trouble came to the Pony Express riders it would be in the country around Virginia City. Here were concentrated the worst ruffians in the West, mainly the notorious Silver Gang who took toll of much of the traffic along the western highway, and also the Nevada Indians who could be reckoned as a menace.

About noon that day a breed youth came in to the station with a message for Ja-Kines. It took them some time to realize that the callow, half-witted lad wanted Jack Irons, but when they did they showed him into the new, pitch-pine office on the outskirts of Carson City.

The breed boy delivered his message. It was brief. He said: 'A fellar told me for to tell Ja-Kines that him Pony Express won't go through Virginie City no time. Him say Ja-Kines not big 'nough man to stop him, no sir.'

The message wasn't very clear, but coupled with the news from Senator Gwin, it left Irons in no doubt as to its origin and perhaps even the purpose behind it.

The mocking, confident — too-confident — Rowlands had sent that message through to him. It was a dare. Rowlands wanted to get Irons away from this rest station in Carson City, wanted to lure him out on to the rough mountain trail away from the protection of more law-abiding citizens. And he succeeded.

Irons at once saddled up Black Lightning and rode out. That gang was going to try to disrupt the mail service. He still couldn't understand who would benefit by such a manouvre, and it certainly didn't seem in Rowlands' interests to do so. But Rowlands was using the threat to bring Irons out on to the open trail where he could settle accounts with him. He rode out because it was his duty to ensure that the mail got through.

He also went out because he wanted to settle with the man who had recently emerged as such a vicious enemy — a man who, by his conduct more than anything else, betrayed his guilt of the crime against poor Belle Storr long ago.

Irons decided that if trouble came it would be on the stretch between Virginia and Carson cities. Here the Pony Express left the winding trail that the wagons took through the Sierras, and instead went by a prospector's route into the mountains. There was little traffic nowadays on this old trail, and it was a wild and difficult piece of country to negotiate. Still it saved several miles by cutting across the wide-curving wagon trail, and miles were important in this mail service.

He rode the length of this trail, with its isolated way station — a hut where two men looked after three fine horses — right in the middle of the desolate country. The men hadn't seen any suspicious characters about the place, so after warning them to keep their guns ready, Irons rode on into Virginia City.

On the day that the first riders were due, simultaneously, to leave St. Joseph in the east, and Sacramento on the western seaboard, Irons rode to a hill that gave a fine view for twenty miles back into the Sierras. There he dismounted and sat and watched the trail. His nerves were tingling at the thought that right now the most romantic race in history had begun — right now all along a nineteen hundred mile trail over prairie, desert and mountains, men were waiting to pick up the mails as they came hurtling in, to bring them at breakneck speed as fast as gallant horseflesh could carry them on to the next relay station.

It was an enterprise to quicken the blood and excite the calmest of men, and this day even Jack Irons wasn't so cool.

Very late that afternoon, far away along the white ribbon of the mountain trail, he saw a fast-moving speck which resolved in time into the figure of a rider and his mount.

He watched it until he was certain that it was the first west-bound Pony Express rider — saw it pull into the West Carson City way station for a change of horses, then with no more than ten seconds delay for the change over, the mail carrier was thundering along the trail again.

Irons mounted now and began to ride ahead along the trail, until the galloping rider gradually caught up with him. Irons raced with him to the next way station, the one right in the Tahoe Mountains, keeping him guard and company over this wild stretch of land.

Then he rode on with him on the next leg of the journey to Virginia City, gradually falling behind because his own horse was too heavily equipped to ride against that unencumbered mount.

And nothing happened. The mail went through without any attempt at a hold-up on anyone's part.

It puzzled Irons. He'd been told that the mail wouldn't get through, and yet no attempt had been made to stop the first east-bound Pony Express rider. It worried him, because it didn't make sense.

He tried to console himself with the thought that the important thing was for the pony riders to get through safely, and this one had ridden triumphantly eastwards with the mail, and yet he was left uneasy.

He had no illusions about Rowlands. Rowlands didn't make threats that he didn't intend to carry out.

He kept off the track for the next three days. There was no sense in deliberately inviting attack now that the mail had gone through. And then it was time for the second rider to make the eastward dash.

The second Atlantic-Coast mail run was scheduled for three days after the first one. By this time Irons calculated that the first rider to have left St. Joseph would be near to Fort Laramie, in Wyoming, seven hundred miles on the way to the Pacific Coast. In less than a week that racing relay would be up to Virginia City, bringing mail faster than it had ever been brought before across the American continent.

Irons repeated his tactics of three days previously. He rode to the same mountain top and stood watch over the trail. When the second Pony Express man came thundering into view, Irons went down to the trail and gradually let the rider catch up with him, and then kept him company for the last couple of miles into the Tahoe Mountain way station.

This time he felt sure that attack would come when they rode out on to that wild trail towards Virginia City, and he rode with his big Colt clutched grimly in his right hand.

The second, grim-faced, intent jockey-rider gradually drew away from Irons, because his horse was fresh and eager to stride out. Irons let him distance him, still able to cover him for a long time along that trail, and when finally the Pony Express man rode out of sight he was so near to Virginia City that Irons knew him to be safe.

It was a very puzzled and quite worried Jack Irons who rested his horse that night in Virginia City. The second east-bound delivery of mail had gone safely through — at least, safely through this stretch of dangerous trail. And in view of Rowlands' threat this didn't make sense. Rowlands hadn't even made any attempt to attack the Pony Express.

Irons gave it up and went to sleep.

Three days later the third rider went through unharmed. By now Irons began to feel that Rowlands had sent that threat through merely to make him lose a lot of sleep, and yet it didn't seem like the man to do that.

Now the great moment was approaching when they should see the first rider bearing the west-bound mail. Anticipating that he might be ahead of schedule, Irons was in Virginia City to look out for him two days ahead of schedule. Ten days was the schedule for the complete run from St. Joe to the coast, and just under nine-and-a-half days to Virginia City. Irons was there on the afternoon of the seventh day.

The town was agog with excitement. Bets were being freely laid. Some said that the mail wouldn't get through — there were too many perils on a route close on two thousand miles over some of the roughest country on earth. Most were optimistic enough to think it would come through, but not in ten days. The bets were being laid on the probable time of arrival in Virginia City.

When they learned that Irons thought it might be quite a bit ahead of time, the rough miners got ribald at his expense. He didn't mind it; he knew the strength of the organization that he had helped to build up. And he watched the east road patiently all that afternoon and evening, and dozed all the night on a bunk in the rest station in the centre of the town.

Next day he rode into the mountains along the Carson City trail, so that he could see far out along the plain of the Great Basin. But he was disappointed, and with darkness rode in again to Virginia City.

Around five in the morning, with dawn creeping into the sky, he was awakened by an excited shout. He shot from the bunk, ready booted and clothed for the trail. The two stable hands were already leading out the fresh horse and the relief rider was tumbling out down the steps towards it, ready and eager to go.

Irons didn't waste time on saddling. He ran Black Lightning out into the street and mounted. Someone was shouting from an upper storey: 'I c'n see him. It's the Express rider. Glory be, he got through ahead of time!' Half a day ahead of schedule over a course of seventeen hundred and fifty miles!

Half-dressed men came surging into the street, more excited than if a new Comstock Lode had been discovered. They started to cheer when the rider was a mile out along the trail from town, a mere cloud of dust that rolled rapidly in towards them. And when the rider came swooping down towards the rest station, there was pandemonium among the spectators. Guns started popping, to add to the cheers, and then men brought their horses out and rode down in a roaring throng to watch the change-over.

It took seconds. The weary rider, who had travelled from the middle of the Great Basin desert all during the night, slipped from his horse as it was caught by one of the stable men. With a quick movement he dragged off the *mochila* — that square of leather to which were attached four *cantinas* containing the precious letters in their oiled silk wrappers — and flung it across the saddle of the fresh horse. Instantly the new rider sprang up, whipped his horse into speed and thundered away up the winding prospector trail through the mountains towards Carson City.

The change-over had been quick, but by now Jack Irons was about a mile ahead of the new rider. He rode steadily, to permit the Pony Express man to catch up with him, employing his tactics of previous occasions. Gradually they drew level, and then Irons let the rider get ahead along that wild, brush-bordered scar of a track. He knew he could keep him in sight until the change-over at the way station in the Tahoe hills, and would overtake him while the exchange of mounts was being made.

Circumstances thus saved Jack Irons' life, for if he had raced into the way station along with the Pony Express rider, as he had done on the two previous occasions, both would have been shot down when the firing opened. This time, though, to conserve his big, ranging horse, Irons was two hundred yards down the trail when the first shot loosed off and brought the mail rider toppling from his saddle.

Afterwards, seeing how the ambush was prepared, Irons realized that he must have been closely watched on those east-bound runs of the Express, and his enemies had decided that the Tahoe Mountain way station was the ideal place to put an end to the mail experiment — and himself.

Irons saw the Pony Express rider sway, then fall off his galloping horse, to roll inanimately in the dust of the trail. The horse, with its precious *mochila* of mail, careered northwards into the bush, at the back of the way station.

Then the sharp crack of a rifle hit his ears and white smoke lifted from a point at a bend in the trail facing up towards him.

Irons realized in that same moment that the fresh horse which should have been standing, held by two stable men, ready for the change-over, wasn't on the trail. Neither were the stable men. It looked as though the ambushers were in control of this important changing station.

Irons at once swung his mount off the trail. Just in time! A ragged fusillade of lead came screeching up from a dozen hidden assailants, cutting into the new-budding bushes as he jumped into them. Then for a second he was safely covered. Hoarse voices shouted, and it seemed that there was chagrin in them, and someone was being abused loudly by a bellowing voice that seemed familiar. Irons felt that that first shot which had downed the Pony Express rider and given him, Irons, warning, shouldn't have been fired so early. Now the impetuous assassin was being upbraided for giving Irons a chance to make his escape.

But the cattleman didn't keep heading north into the scrub. Back by the way station that exhausted pony with its precious load of mail would be standing. Irons didn't intend to let that mail get into the ambushers' hands — more, he vowed that the mail was going through on time!

He flung himself out of the saddle within a dense clump of stunted oaks and high, prickly thorns. He knew that he wouldn't need to tie his mount, pretty well blown after that fast ride up from Virginia City, so he left it with the reins trailing over its head. The rest would do Black Lightning a lot of good.

He ran off through the scattered trees towards the way station. There was a lot of noise coming from it. As he broke from cover he was in time to see two mounted men come riding up with the tired Express pony between them. Irons took a risk and kept on running, gambling on everyone's interest in the captured pony.

The riders went out of sight round the log hut that was the way station, enabling Irons to run in close behind them. He halted, trying to control his heavy breathing so that the sound wouldn't give him away, and then he took off his hat and peered cautiously round the corner of the station.

The trail in front of the building was crowded with men and horses. Irons didn't recognize any at first — they were rough-clothed, unshaven, hard-faced deperadoes, the kind that any man can hire for any piece of thuggery, provided he has money enough to pay their price.

Then the men parted in response to that bellow that sounded so familiar. A man started to step across to the sweat-lathered pony. Irons just caught a glimpse of him — then he wheeled, his gun lifting.

Someone was crouching behind him, coming stealthily up.

It was Rowlands.

At the movement, Rowlands made a headlong dive for cover, opening fire and shouting at the same time. Irons fired — and missed. Then Rowlands fired again. It drove the cattleman back on to the trail — the only way he could go. Right on to the guns of the desperadoes and their boss.

Irons reeled round the corner, stumbled over two bound and gagged forms — the stable men. Then he was facing the gang. He was also facing the man who seemed to be their boss, even though he had been told that Rowlands had recruited them.

The boss was a small, angry man, with vicious, snapping brown eyes and a perpetual snarl upon his lips.

Jud Awker, the freight operator between San Francisco and Salt Lake City.

The sudden crash of guns was unexpected by the gang, and it gave Irons a split-second chance to act. He dived forward, his gun flaming at the men who had so treacherously shot down the unarmed mail rider. They flung themselves down and away from the line of fire, and that left the startled mail pony unattended on the trail.

Irons leapt in leap-frog manner into the saddle, his heels instantly kicking to urge the tired horse into a gallop.

Pistols were lifting and roaring off all around him, as the tough-looking hold-up men rolled and sighted from the dust. Lead screeched close by him, but the plunging, frightened horse had upset their aim.

It was spent from its mad race along the rough mountain trail, but fear gave it momentary strength, and it leapt forward; a slight pressure of the cattleman's knees while he fired to disturb the aim of his assailants brought the plunging beast and rider within the cover of the log hut.

Men's voices roared behind him. They'd be shouting to take up the chase on horseback, recognizing that he couldn't go far on this weary horse. And Jud Awker's voice lifted above all the rest.

Jud Awker . . . Irons began to understand now. The Pony Express represented a threat to the Awker interests, because with it, ultimately, would come the powerful Russell, Majors & Waddell firm, who would compete for freight with the Awker company.

But if Awker could prevent the vital west-bound mail from going through, then the service which had cost so much to establish would collapse, and the Leavenworth firm would, presumably, pull out and cease to be competitors on the west coast.

The Pony Express seemed as though it would have a hazardous life in the near future, fighting for its existence against this determined little freight-haulier and his gang.

Rowlands . . . He was cleverer, more crafty than Awker. No doubt he had cunningly inspired this plan, but had done it to encompass his own ends. He had intended to use Awker's gang to wipe out a formidable enemy, a man who guessed that he was the killer of a girl back east.

But, so far, the plan had failed.

Irons heard a thunder of hooves behind him as he nursed his flagging mount through the scattered trees on the hillside. They would catch up with him in a matter of minutes, he guessed.

Then he saw the thick patch of trees and bushes in which Black Lightning stood. This pause would have given the gallant beast time to recover a little from the hard ride along the trail.

Irons rode up, leaping for the ground and in the same movement dragging the leather *mochila* off behind him. Black Lightning reared, startled by the sight of this bounding man with the flapping leather swinging in his left hand. Then the *mochila* was across the bare back, and Irons was vaulting on to it, his legs between the box-like *cantinas* containing the mail.

Black Lightning streaked out from cover as if it was the first time this day that he had borne a rider. A shout of dismay rose from the rapidly overtaking gang behind him. Then guns blatted after him, only these were short-range Colts, because it is nearly impossible to use a rifle with effect from the back of a rapidly-moving horse.

They did no damage, even though he

was within range when he first rode out on Black Lightning.

Irons put his horse across some level ground that terminated in a steep rise that would eventually lead out on to the Carson City trail. Gallantly the horse stretched out, responsive to his urgings, and began to leave the pursuers farther and farther behind.

Irons knew, though, that they would have to slacken pace when they hit the steep rise, and that would give the pursuers a chance to race up within pistol range again. He drew out his Colt, and rode looking back over his shoulder. His horse started to climb, and at once Black Lightning's pace slackened. The gang shouted in hoarse triumph and seemed to come up with a rush.

Irons held his fire even after they had opened up on him — held it until it was almost too late. And he noticed even at that moment that neither Rowlands nor Jud Awker were up in the forefront of the pursuit. They were men who preferred to leave the dirty work to others.

Suddenly he fired and went on firing. He hated to do it, but he knew his life was at stake. He fired straight at the leading horse, a wild-eyed bay. It seemed to collapse, hurling its rider into a shapeless huddle right in the path of those racing hoofs.

That stopped the pursuit. All in one second there was a tremendous pile up of a dozen horses and their riders, as the gang, unable to stop themselves, rode on to the stricken bay.

Rowlands, in the rear, pulled up and started to use his rifle, but he was cursing with fury for he knew that he had been beaten.

Like a great black cat, Irons' horse went leaping up the slope; it gained the trail above, blew deeply through its wide-open nostrils, and settled down to the nine-mile run into Carson City. Irons let him go easily. The mail was half a day ahead of schedule, and he had no fear of pursuit now.

He even walked the horse into Carson City. Black Lightning had saved his life with that gallant sprint after the long run in on the Virginia trail. He wasn't going to burst its heart unnecessarily.

They stood and cheered him in as he walked wearily along Carson City's main street to where a fresh horse stood ready saddled for the trail. In response to the shouted questions he called back that there had been an attempted hold-up and the Virginia City rider had been shot and killed.

He slipped from his horse, dragging the *mochila* with him. There was still sixty miles of trail to the Pacific end of the route in Sacramento, and for a moment Irons toyed with the idea of going through with the run himself. It would have been a glorious moment, to have come riding through with the first Pony Express mail from the east.

Then he saw a thin face that he remembered. It belonged to a man who had once been clerk in a stage line's office in San Francisco. He'd thrown up his job to beg from Irons the chance to ride for the Pony Express, and when he'd been told that all the riders they needed had been engaged, he'd taken on the job of stable man and way station attendant so as to be part of this thrilling Pony Express organization.

Irons said: 'Guess I'm too big for a Pony Express rider.' His weight would prove a severe strain to the horses along the Sierra Nevada trail. That white, thin face watched him in a way that hurt. Irons said, casually: 'Reckon you'd better take the mail to Sacramento, brother.'

The man gulped, then his mouth opened and shut. Then he jumped for the horse. He was the proudest man in all America at that moment. He was to carry the mail on the last leg of the journey across the American continent — the fastest relay race the world had ever known. Sacramento would be *en fête* to receive him; he would be the hero of the hour. This was the most wonderful hour of his life!

The Carson City mail was dragged out of the *cantina*, the Sacramento mail put in. Then the *mochila* was flung across the saddle of the eager, excited horse. The thin-faced man leapt into the saddle.

Carson City went crazy, seeing that horseman ride away as if all the furies in hell were after him. Then they went to the saloons to celebrate and settle their bets. There was no working for Carson City that day.

The Pony Express was a reality. A seemingly wild idea had been proved sound. Mail could be brought from the Atlantic to the Pacific in little more than ten days . . .

Only Irons sat alone on the verandah of the way station, his headquarters on the Sierra Nevada trail. He felt curiously depressed after the triumph of the day. Reaction had set in and he found himself looking pessimistically to the future.

He knew it was going to be a fight to keep the trail open for the Pony Express, here in the Sierras. Big-money interests wanted to break it and keep out the competition that must follow if the Russell firm made it a success. There would be savage fighting to stop the riders from coming in, and he couldn't bank on having luck on his side all the time.

And somehow he felt lonely, felt as though he were alone in this fight. His thoughts strayed to Ann Caudry, and he sighed as he remembered those long, cold hours on the trail back east — long and cold, but delicious in his memory. And that was what hurt him most, to think there was almost a continent between him and the girl he loved, and that never again might he see her.

'She'll forget me,' he thought, rising, a sense of frustration urging him into action. And he thought that he could never forget her.

The stable man came out to take the mail down to the Carson City post office. 'Company's mail all sorted,' he proclaimed. The company's mail seemed to consist of one letter.

Irons asked, surprised: 'For me?'

It was.

He opened it and read: '*Poor mother died last week. I am heart-broken. I want to see you, Jack. Can I come to Carson City?*'

It was signed: '*Ann.*'

The blood seemed to roar through Irons' head. His hand trembled as he gripped that letter. Then he shouted: 'What time does the east-bound mail come in?' And he was exulting.

Thanks to the magnificent Pony Express his answer could reach Ann in little more than a week. He ran for writing materials, and when he'd written the simple sentence: '*I want you to come — Jack,*' he raced for a horse.

The Tahoe Mountain way station had to be readied for the rider going east that afternoon.

Iron Jack was in action again!

We do hope that you have enjoyed reading this large print book.

Did you know that all of our titles are available for purchase?

We publish a wide range of high quality large print books including:
**Romances, Mysteries, Classics
General Fiction
Non Fiction and Westerns**

Special interest titles available in large print are:
**The Little Oxford Dictionary
Music Book, Song Book
Hymn Book, Service Book**

Also available from us courtesy of Oxford University Press:
**Young Readers' Dictionary
(large print edition)
Young Readers' Thesaurus
(large print edition)**

For further information or a free brochure, please contact us at:
**Ulverscroft Large Print Books Ltd.,
The Green, Bradgate Road, Anstey,
Leicester, LE7 7FU, England.
Tel:** (00 44) **0116 236 4325**
Fax: (00 44) **0116 234 0205**

LAST STAGE FROM HELL'S MOUTH

Derek Rutherford

Sam Cotton is the last person anyone in the New Mexico town of Hope would have suspected of wrong-doing. All that changes, however, when he is seen riding away hell for leather from a scene of robbery and death. Though the victims' families save him from a lynching, once the judge arrives in town, Sam will stand trial for his life — with only his father believing in his innocence . . .

SKELETON PASS

John Russell Fearn

Prospecting for gold in the mountains, Pan Warlow discovers a bonanza — but does not live to enjoy his good fortune. Accidentally blowing himself up, he brings about a cataclysmic avalanche. Now he lies buried beneath a pile of rocks in Skeleton Pass — alongside $200,000 worth of gold belonging to wealthy banker Lanning Mackenzie. Lanning's daughter Flora is determined to find the treasure, aided by her Aunt Belinda, Dick Crespin and Black Moon. But she is in danger from the notorious outlaw Loupe Vanquera . . .

DEAD MAN'S CANYON

Terrell L. Bowers

After the Civil War, former ranger Nicolas Kilpatrick and his fellow ex-soldiers continue to deploy their skills, protecting settlers from Indian attacks and tracking down gangs of robbers and rustlers. In the wake of a shootout with the murderous Maitland Guerrillas, a dying bandit offers Nick information on the gang's leader — in exchange for a promise that his soon-to-be-widow will be taken care of. Setting off to chase down Frank Maitland and keep his vow, Nick heads out to Laramie . . .

LONGHORN JUSTICE

Will DuRey

Cattle baron Nat Erdlatter has built his empire by taking what he wants, then ruthlessly holding on to it. Even now, with the Homestead Act encouraging people to claim their own portions of land, he believes that his needs take precedence over the government's decrees. But times are changing, and the citizens of nearby Enterprise are angered by his latest callous act — none more so than his ranch hands Clem Rawlings and Gus Farley, who become embroiled in an affair that can only lead to violence and danger . . .

BADMAN SHERIFF

Simon Webb

When the citizens of Coopers Creek elect Ned Turner as their sheriff, they are blind to the deadly mistake being made. For Turner is a lawless rogue seeking to exploit the position for his own advantage. It will be left to mild-mannered baker Jack Crawley to set things right. But can he rescue his town from the worst badman sheriff Montana has ever known?